Voice

of the

Lost

Medair: Book 2

by Andrea K Höst

All characters in this publication
are fictitious and any resemblance
to real persons, living or dead,
is purely coincidental.

Voice of the Lost
© 2011 Andrea K Höst. All rights reserved.
ISBN: 978-0-9808789-2-9
EBook ISBN: 978-0-9808789-3-6
www.andreakhost.com
Cover art: Julie Dillon

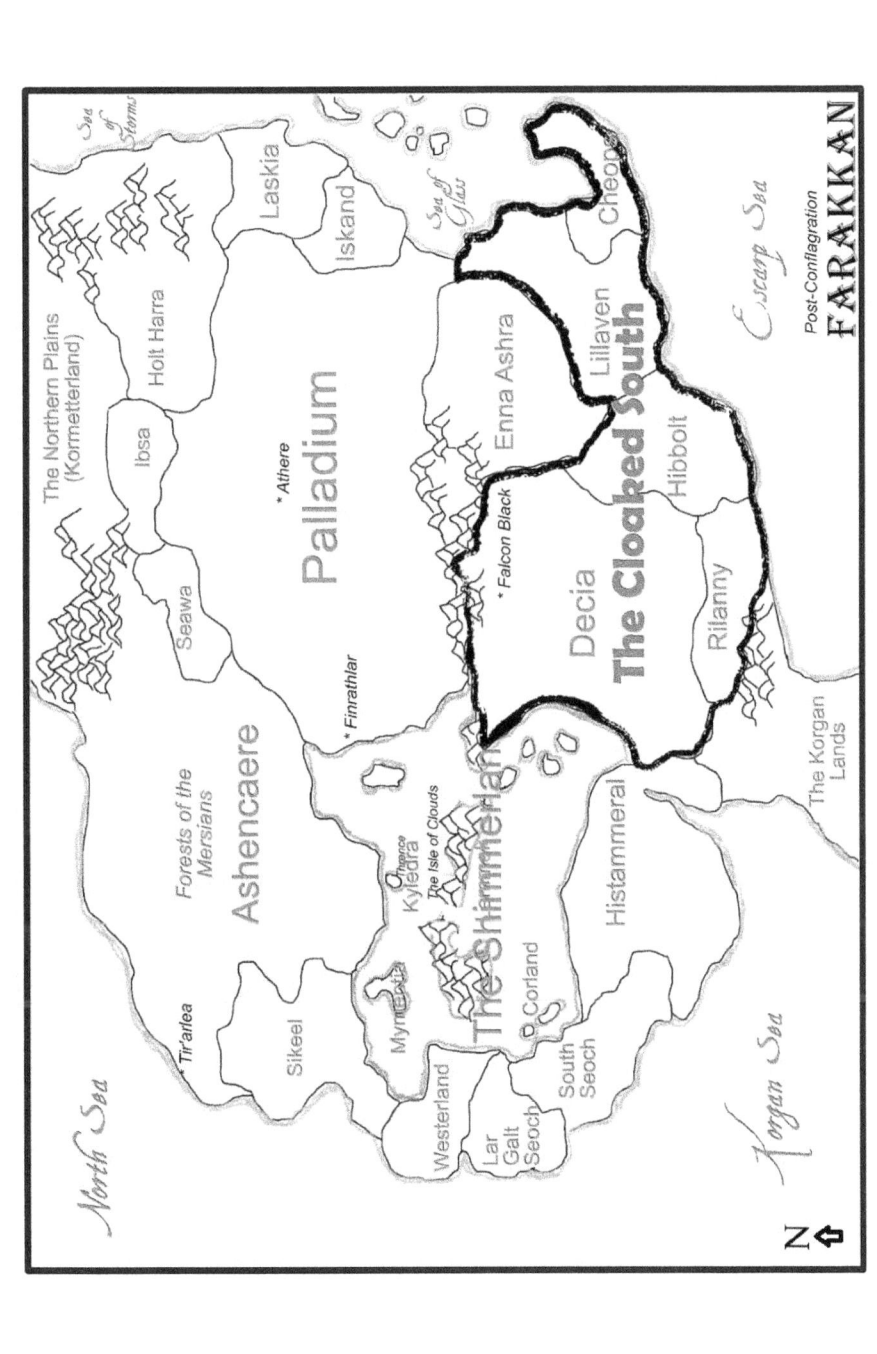

FARAKKAN

Post-Conflagration

ONE

Hands gripping her wrists.

Jolted from sleep, Medair an Rynstar, displaced herald of a fallen Empire, opened her eyes in time to see a wide cushion descend. Brocade and too many inches of stuffing made it impossible to breathe, and she tried to turn her head, for a moment too astonished for more. Was it Medarists already, come to punish her for not being the hero they had expected? For the crime of not hating enough? Then fear overcame shock and she writhed against the hands which held her. Unable to free her wrists, she reared back and kicked.

Her feet flailed at nothing, then someone caught hold of her left leg, pinning it down. *At least three attackers.*

Medair had known this would come, had known that anyone loyal to the old Atherian Empire would hate her unrelentingly for aiding the descendants of the Ibisian invaders, and would not think five hundred years of interbreeding and the threat of indiscriminate slaughter enough to muddy the waters of enmity. But she had not anticipated assassins the same afternoon she had given up the Horn, and certainly not while she was shut away in the apartments of an Ibisian of the highest rank: Cor-Ibis.

Panicked by the tightness growing in her chest, she cried out for help, but the cushion muffled sound as readily as air. Despite her forestalled attempt at suicide a few decems earlier, Medair did not find being murdered an acceptable solution to her problems, and struggled to think her way out of this trap. The only set-spell she'd prepared in weeks was the fire-light charm, but the finger snap release produced no response. It had lapsed.

Bright spots began to speck the blackness before her eyes, but still she looked for escape, going limp for a count of five in hopes of lulling them. Only the hold on her legs relaxed, but that was enough, and she snapped her feet up, this time curling almost double in her effort to strike at her captors. Muscles burned with strain, but she came into contact with the arm of the person who held her right wrist and pushed out with her foot, succeeding in thrusting that one backward. Something broke – jostled from the table beside her bed? – and the pressure on the cushion lapsed, allowing her to steal a single breath. But no more.

"*Hold* her!" one ordered in an angry whisper. It was a voice she knew. A woman's voice, muffled but familiar, made outlandish by circumstances. Jedda las Theomain.

That did not make sense. Keris las Theomain was Ibisian, a friend of their ruler, Kier Inelkar, and had been with Cor-Ibis' group during his search for the stolen rahlstones which had led to his path crossing Medair's. The Keris knew perfectly well Medair had given the rahlstones and then the Horn of Farak, the very weapon Medair had sought to destroy the Ibisian invaders, to their descendants. With the city under siege, why were the people she had betrayed her past to help trying to kill her?

Writhing impotently, Medair struggled for another breath. The third assailant was practically sitting on her feet. She couldn't begin to guess why Jedda las Theomain, why any Ibisian, would sneak into her room and attack her. It was everyone *else* who had reason to kill Medair an Rynstar.

A tap on the door, then the voice of Cor-Ibis' ward:

"Medair?"

"Ileaha!" Medair shouted, or tried to, struggling against a rising wave of grey. The effort left her chest stretched and empty, and did not seem to have produced noise to rival an infuriated mouse. Ileaha tapped on the door again.

"Something broke. Are you all right?"

A strained silence was all the answer she had, while Medair struggled to suck air through the scratchy brocade. Then, a click.

The weight sitting on Medair's feet was gone in a bound. There was an indrawn breath, a scuffle, and the door slammed shut. But Ileaha did not seem to be easy prey. Something else fell, there was more scuffling, then Ileaha's voice rose, urgent and imperative:

"*Liak! Mehtra! To me!*"

It seemed, from the grey place Medair was sinking into, that Ileaha did not wait for the arrival of the special guards assigned to Cor-Ibis, but dashed toward the person wielding the cushion. The bedside table collapsed as two bodies landed upon it. Medair, the cushion wrenched away from her face, gulped air.

The man holding her left wrist was Ibisian, his bleached skin and white hair showing no hint of Farakkian blood. Blue eyes narrowing, he let go only to draw a knife. Medair barely got her hands up before he slashed toward her throat. The sturdy fabric of her uniform gave her some protection, but red lines opened across the back of her right wrist and the palm of her left. Then a splintered table leg hurtled past Medair and hit the man in the face. His free hand went to his cheek, but he again thrust at Medair, frantically now, as if killing her were more important to him than his own life. Medair snatched up the abandoned cushion as a makeshift shield, and feathers puffed into the air.

Ileaha, ash blonde hair flying, left Jedda las Theomain crumpled on the floor, and launched across the bed. She hit the man feet first, the knife scoring her boot before it clattered away. She landed on top of him and had him face down with hands wrenched behind his back in one swift whirl. The third intruder tried to make his escape and staggered into the arms of Liak ar Haedrin and another Farakkian woman in the Cor-Ibis livery.

Suddenly the room was full of people. Guards, maids, Avahn. Medair, head swirling, dropped the gutted cushion. She picked a feather from the roof of her mouth, and tried to smile at her rescuer. It seemed a better option than bursting into tears.

"I really can't imagine you as a secretary, Ileaha," she said, voice thin and creaking. "I'm glad you decided otherwise."

"So am I," Ileaha replied, staring at Jedda las Theomain. There was no sign of movement and the woman's long limbs lay in awkward positions. Then Ileaha glanced at Medair and her eyes widened. "He did cut you!"

"Vel will bring bandages," Avahn said. Cor-Ibis' heir made a brief, commanding gesture to someone at the door, then nodded at Ileaha with approval. "I think I've lost any right to deride your weapons-skill, 'Leaha."

Ileaha lifted her chin, then nodded back, adding only the faintest searching glance to show that she had not quite fully transitioned from the doubt-filled girl Medair had met at an inn in Kyledra. A mixed-blood minor mage raised as ward of a family dominated by powerful full-Ibisian adepts, she was unlikely to quickly forget Avahn's careless taunts, or the weight of charity driving her toward a dutiful but dull career. Saving Medair was a large stride into the profession of her choice.

"Show me your hands," Avahn ordered, and produced a sturdy kerchief when Medair unclasped her injured wrist. It was not enough to stem the bleeding, but it at least stopped her dripping, freeing him to turn his attention to the man on the floor.

"Sit him up." He studied the captive, an Ibisian of forty or so years, already withdrawing behind a mask of icy control. "Who are you?"

The man just sat there, face set. Avahn's eyes flashed, but he reined himself back, drawing on the Ibisian calm supposedly bequeathed by 'cold blood'.

"Do you know him, Liak?" he asked, turning to the gathering at the door.

"No, Kerin," the red-headed woman replied. "This one is Felden, of the household since a year past, but I have never seen this other before."

"Ah." Avahn's gaze rested on the young man bracketed by Kel ar Haedrin and her companion, then he turned to look at Jedda las Theomain's body. "Search them."

This was swiftly accomplished and revealed only that Jedda was definitely dead. Ileaha pressed her lips together at the news, but didn't otherwise react.

"Did they speak to you, Medair?"

"No," Medair replied, tightening Avahn's now soaked kerchief around her palm. "I'm not altogether sure why an Ibisian would be trying to kill me."

"It had to be done," said the man who had cut her, his voice precise and unapologetic. "Keris las Theomain saw clearly the threat you pose. It will not happen. You can be sure of that."

"What threat?" Medair asked blankly, but the man just tightened his lips.

"Take them somewhere less intrusive," Avahn ordered. "And clear the door. Where is Vel?"

"Here, Kerin." An elderly Ibisian woman came forward, a collection of salves, needles and bandages neatly laid out on the tray she carried.

Avahn left Medair to the ministrations of the attendant, while Jedda las Theomain's body was removed. The cut on the back of Medair's right wrist and hand wasn't bad, but her left palm was scored deeply across the base of the thumb. The woman called Vel tended it with a mixture of stitches and a casting to hurry the healing. Medair wondered why Jedda had started with a cushion instead of the knife, and tried not to picture that awakening.

"There will be no loss of function, Kerin," the attendant told Avahn when he returned. She wrapped an injury which now looked days old. "It did not touch the tendons."

"That's as well." Avahn glanced around the room, at blood-specked feathers and broken furniture. "We guarded you poorly, Medair. We thought you would be at risk from the Hold, or from Medarists, not our own kind."

"What *is* the Hold, Avahn? I've often wanted to ask."

Avahn, after a startled pause, reverted to his more usual persona, laughing. "You don't know, do you? We were convinced, at one time, that you were an agent of the Hold, or at least their tool. We never came even close to guessing the truth." He laid the cushion on the bed and placed the knife neatly upon it. "The Hold of the Emperor – it started as a resistance movement in the time after the *Niadril* Kier's death. Certain of the Farak-lar nobles who had surrendered attempted to retake the throne in the name of the surviving Corminevar, Princess Alaire.

"Their first open move was an attempt to kill Kierash Elvalar, Kier Ieskar's newborn heir. A serious miscalculation: the Princess would not allow her daughter to be murdered, no matter the child's father. Alaire never supported them, and it ended in executions. But the Hold itself still flourished. For centuries they have worked behind the scenes, pulling the strings of those such as the

Medarists, weakening from within and allying without. Playing their games."

"I'm surprised you let me travel with you, thinking me one of these puppeteers."

"Owing life-debt, glimpsing the secrets you held? We were not inclined to trust you, Medair, but you were far too interesting a study not to pursue. Besides, there are factions within the Hold, and some no longer consider the Ibis-lar vermin to be hunted from Farak's breast."

"And Jedda las Theomain?" she asked, in a lowered voice. "She was certainly no agent of the Hold."

"No." Avahn lost his incisive air and looked worried. "I don't know where this has come from. She could not possibly have thought the Horn of Farak false. No-one could mistake that power. Unless she thought that, despite everything you have done for us, you would inevitably be used by those who band against us." He did not sound convinced, meeting her eyes with forthright concern. "Liak tells me that one of the attackers – Felden – has purist sympathies. I don't know why they would want you dead, but that may be where this comes from. Though for Keris las Theomain to be a purist, when her links to the Kier are so strong–" He shook his head. "The thoughts of those who would keep the Ibis-lar bloodline pure must be strange indeed to find reason to kill someone who has preserved us."

Medair smiled thinly. "I have become unpopular in all corners, it seems. Perhaps I can hope that the Medarists will stop taking my name."

"Or learn–" He stopped. "I had best see to our captives. There is not much time before sunset, and I wish to speak with Liak about having them questioned before we go to the outer wall."

"To ask them whether more will come after me?"

"To ask them why."

With a formal inclination of his head, Avahn left once more, leaving Medair to the wreckage of the room. Testament that she was not safe even from the Ibisians.

She should have left sooner, found some way out of the city despite the army at the gates, and rested only after sufficient distance allowed her to return to anonymity, to leave the mistakes of Medair an Rynstar behind her.

"The same mistake, all over again."

She had slept after finding the Horn of Farak, and lost the chance to use the Horn to destroy the invading Ibisian army. Today she had let escape slip through her fingers, and would have to face the consequence of her choices. The Horn would be used on a Farakkian army, one which claimed to represent a true Corminevar heir, one not tainted by Ibisian blood. People would die, and those deaths would be laid firmly at her feet. What did it matter that she was sworn to defend Athere, that her act would save the descendants of the oldest Atherian families, that even the most pure-blooded Ibisian families now thought themselves Palladian? Time had muddied everything, making it impossible to do anything, to do nothing, without in some way betraying her oaths, and herself.

Inevitably a traitor.

Medair flexed her hands within their bandages then retrieved her satchel from beneath the bed and undressed, carefully folding the damaged pearl-gray uniform and tucking it away. She would never wear it again. She was oath-breaker, placeless and lost. Herald no longer.

Two

Sunset saw thousands gathered along the southern reach of Athere's outermost wall. The army beyond had spent the hours since its abrupt appearance positioning for attack, and casting. Impossible at such distance to distinguish the exact nature of so many spells but, as Avahn remarked, the sheer number and strength told them all too much. The Ibisians' long supremacy in matters of magic seemed to have been lost, like so many other things, in the transformation wrought by the Conflagration: wild magic slipped from control.

But magic-rich armies appearing overnight was only one of too many changes. The Conflagration had not left the land seared and blackened, but it had altered Farakkan to the point where Athere's defenders' greatest disadvantage was lack of knowledge. The attackers and the spells they might use in this transformed world were a puzzle the Ibisians did not have time to unravel.

Yesterday Medair had stood safely invisible among a less orderly crowd, watching as the city's most powerful adepts constructed a shield to hold back the Conflagration. Today, unmasked and under escort, she could not fail to notice the ripple of attention which followed her. Abandoning her uniform would not grant her anonymity.

There'd been a time when she'd enjoyed people looking at her. Proud little herald.

"Were you on the wall, Ileaha?" she asked. "When they raised the shield?"

"No," Ileaha's attention was on Avahn as he slipped through the knot of people surrounding the Kier. "I was on Fasthold."

Ileaha must have stood with Cor-Ibis while he served as keystone for that formidable casting. And now he was mere feet away, at the Kier's elbow, turning in response to a word from Avahn. Looking back at her.

Before the world had been transformed by flame, and before Medair had slept away five hundred years, there had been two brothers, their island kingdom consumed by disastrously misused wild magic. The younger, Illukar, died ending that Blight. Medair had met his young daughter, in the company of the elder brother, Ieskar, the Ibisian Kier, who she hated above all things for deciding to conquer Athere rather than accept the Emperor's offer of refuge.

The man on this wall, tall and too pale, with his ridiculous length of hair neatly bound in braids, was the fourth to be named Illukar las Cor-Ibis. Descended from the first Illukar's child, with no drop of Farakkian blood to sully him, he was the epitome of a traditional Ibisian: measured, powerful and reserved. Medair was ashamed to be so glad he had survived acting as keystone for the shield.

That, above all else, made her every decision suspect. Had she given the Horn of Farak to the Ibisian Kier, to Ieskar's descendant, because she did not want Illukar las Cor-Ibis to die?

"The Horn is in that chest," Ileaha murmured. "The shielding isn't so complete as that on your satchel, but it serves."

"The air feels thick," Medair said, not certain if that was due to the unbound power lingering in the wake of the Conflagration, or to the enchantments of two armies. "It's different than – different to other sieges."

"Other–" Ileaha's gaze wavered, and the hand she rested on her sword hilt twitched. "It takes some adjustment, knowing who you are, realising what you have seen. I don't imagine that in any of those past battles blood magic would have been used by either side, and I fear that is part of what we are feeling. Look."

She stepped closer to the parapet, but Medair was slow to follow, reluctantly moving to gaze down at what had driven her, finally, to take up her name.

A most orderly army. The Ibisians had been the same way: arraying themselves before the walls of the Empire's cities with care and precision. Five hundred years after Athere fell to the Ibisian invaders, the Decian King, Estarion, used wild magic to give himself the strength to drive them out. Now his forces were placed safely out of the range of combat casting, and in the tinted light there was an almost pleasant symmetry to their serried ranks. Sewn with an even hand among them were giants, near half again as tall as ordinary Farakkians, their horned helmets increasing that height further. Had they been human once, before the transformative power of wild magic had swept over everything outside Athere's shields, and changed their entire world and all its rules?

"Not all blood magic is foul," Ileaha was saying "It's very closely related to the healing arts and, used with care and good conscience, a portion of life force can be sacrificed without permanent injury. But that is not what we feel now, what is stifling the air. If that truly is blood magic, then people are dying out there, before the first blow of this battle has fallen."

"Was he known to use it? The Estarion before the Conflagration?" Medair was finding some slight comfort in Estarion's lack of morals. She had called the invading Ibisians 'White Snakes', thought them cold and greedy, but they had prosecuted their war with an aim to minimise losses, taking advantage of their disproportionate strength in magic to capture their first city without the loss of a single life. Estarion threatened the opposite, promising to slaughter every Ibisian down to the smallest child.

"Known?" Ileaha lifted both hands to measure her lack of certainty. "Not in the world which was mine. But is one who is willing to risk the possible consequences of drawing on wild magic less likely to directly sacrifice lives to his cause?" She lowered her voice. "You – you must not continue to blame this on yourself, Medair. If you had given the rahlstones to Decia instead of us, they still would not have granted Estarion enough strength to take Athere with any surety, let alone place himself before her gates so abruptly. There is every chance he still would have turned to wild magic to gain the strength he lacked."

"Unless he had the Horn," Medair pointed out, and Ileaha fell silent because it was true. The whole reason Medair had set out to find the Horn of Farak was that it promised easy, overwhelming victory; a single weapon to lay low an entire army. Lacking that, Decia's King had summoned wild magic, the temptation of every mage who desired more than they had strength to achieve. The secret of how to do so was supposed to be hidden, locked away, because if wild magic slipped from control it would burn unchecked over all Farakkan. That was a consequence which no-one should have been willing to risk, but without the Horn, Estarion had taken that step. Impossible to predict that the arcane fire he unleashed would not burn the world to dust, but remake it into one where he was well able to bring down the walls of the White City.

With so much changed, what had become of the Corminevar heir Estarion claimed to support? Was he out in that forest of swords? When the Horn was sounded, would Medair be responsible for his death?

The sky faded, and it was a relief not to be so visible. But then Cor-Ibis stopped talking with the Kier and moved several steps closer to Medair. The glow surrounding him – an after-effect of serving as keystone to the shield – grew ever more marked in the gloom, and he made an admirable beacon for those who wanted to stare at the past come to life. He did not speak to Medair, had not said a word directly to her since she had revealed herself. He seemed impossibly Ibisian: cold and distant. How strongly had her actions been influenced by this man? How could someone who so epitomised everything purely Ibis-lar, who reminded her so strongly of Kier Ieskar, draw her as he did?

"MEDAIR AN RYNSTAR."

The voice rolled out of the twilight, turning Medair's name into a wave which crashed across Athere. Medair was not altogether surprised that Estarion chose to address her, that he knew what she had done. For the southern king to underline her betrayal would likely be only one of countless incidents. Assassinations and accusations. The life her conscience had not allowed her to avoid.

"MEDAIR AN RYNSTAR," Estarion repeated, voice thoughtful, contemplative, despite being magnified to an almost painful volume. **"A NAME I HAVE HEARD ALL MY LIFE, IN BALLADS, IN TALES TOLD TO ME WHEN I WAS A CHILD TOO RESTLESS FOR SLEEP. A NAME OF HOPE AND HONOUR. A NAME WHICH MADE A PROMISE."**

"I sense a major casting, *Ekarrel*," Cor-Ibis warned Kier Inelkar. "Something beyond the enhancement of his voice."

Glancing secretly at the Keridahl's cool profile, Medair saw his eyes narrow slightly at Estarion's next words.

"I ENVY YOU."

"He is a showman, this Estarion," Avahn murmured, moving to stand beside Cor-Ibis. "Full of dramatic pauses." He smiled reassuringly at Medair, but in the dim twilight he looked worried.

"THE PALLADIAN EMPIRE, THE GOLDEN AGE OF PEACE. IT SHINES IN OUR PAST, A TIME OF GROWTH WITHOUT STRIFE, OF A SEEKING FOR PERFECTION RATHER THAN POWER. WE WILL NEVER KNOW THE WORLD YOU WERE BORN TO, MEDAIR AN RYNSTAR, BUT WE SHARE A DESIRE TO SEE AN END TO THE WARS WHICH SNATCHED IT AWAY."

"Don't tell me he's going to back down?" someone muttered disbelievingly. Medair barely heard the interjection, eyes fixed unwavering on the stone beneath her feet. Where was Estarion leading? This was not the harangue for which she had steeled herself, but a far crueller attack. She faced the despair which had kept her paralysed this past year. The Empire was gone. Everyone, everything which had been hers. Nothing would ever change that.

"I CAN ONLY GUESS AT YOUR FEELINGS, WHEN YOU RETURNED HERE, TO WHAT HAD BEEN THE HEART OF THE EMPIRE, AND FOUND IT AS IT IS. DID IT NOT WRING YOUR VERY SOUL TO SEE IT? WERE YOU TEMPTED TO USE THE HORN, EVEN THOUGH THE MOMENT WAS LOST?"

Again a pause, serving to underline his last words. She remembered that angry desire all too well.

"I DO NOT NAME YOU ENEMY, MEDAIR AN RYNSTAR. YOU, AS I, SEEK PEACE, AN END TO WAR. YOU FELL INTO THE HANDS OF THE WHITE SNAKES AND LOST PERSPECTIVE, REACTED TO THE MOMENT RATHER THAN THE LARGER PICTURE. THERE WILL BE NO PEACE WHILE A SINGLE COLD SNAKE THINKS TO RULE FARAKKIAN TERRITORY. THERE WILL BE NO END TO WAR UNTIL THE ROT IS CUT OUT. CAN YOU DENY THAT?"

Medair suspected he was right, but shied from the slaughter he seemed to consider the solution. Did Estarion plan to hunt down every Ibisian on Farakkan, after razing Athere? What of those like Ileaha, who were also Farakkian? Or those with barely a drop of cold blood? And yet, and yet– She started to raise a hand to her head, then restrained herself, too aware of all who watched her through the gloom. Ibisians. White Snakes. She would not show weakness before them.

"**AFTER THE BATTLE, SEEK ME OUT, MEDAIR AN RYNSTAR. THERE IS SOMEONE I WISH YOU TO MEET; A TRUE DESCENDANT OF THE ONE TO WHOM YOU GAVE OATH.**"

He was talking of the heir he supported – or used as banner and excuse for war. Said to descend from Verium, her Emperor's son, a line long kept hidden and protected until the moment came to return them too their rightful place on the Silver Throne. And Medair knew very well that it was possible, that Verium had been involved with the woman said to have borne a true Corminevar heir. Had she turned her back on him, this Tarsus, so-called Emperor-in-Exile?

And it was all too long ago, too muddied and tangled. For Kier Inelkar descended from Medair's Emperor as well, and her throne had been won in conquest, making questions of legitimacy secondary. More to the point, thousands of Farakkians, loyal Atherians with no drop of White Snake blood, would give their lives to protect their Kier. To them, Decia was nothing but an invader, and Tarsus an irrelevancy.

Numbness gripped Medair, the crushing weight of impossible choice she had struggled with all year. She shifted her gaze to the box which held what had been meant to be the salvation of the Empire.

"**NOW. INELKAR. HAS IT YET OCCURRED TO YOU THAT THE HORN OF FARAK WILL NOT ANSWER YOUR COLD BLOOD?**"

Estarion chuckled, a rumble of thunder in the night. The glint of fire on metal served as lightning. Out among the massed troops, torches were being lit. They flared like stars, thousands upon thousands of points of light. Medair's attention was briefly torn from the almost mesmeric influence of the metal-bound box. She saw with a shudder that Estarion's army was holding aloft not torches, but burning swords. The wind carried the tang of hot metal, and a faint whisper of words she could not understand. Then Estarion's voice boomed again.

"**WHITE SNAKE, PALE INVADER. YOU BURIED ANY TRACE OF FARAK BENEATH GENERATIONS OF OUTLAND BLOOD. IT IS —**"

"Could he be right?" the Kier asked.

"**— A SOURCE OF AMAZEMENT TO ME THAT YOU COULD HOPE TO USURP —**"

"It is all too possible, *Ekarrel*," Antellar, the Keridahl Alar, replied. "We were not certain what the Horn would do before the Conflagration, let alone in the world we now face.*"*

"**— THIS AS WELL. FARAK WILL NOT ANSWER YOU, INELKAR! THE HORN OF FARAK SERVES THE CHILDREN OF FARAKKAN ALONE! AND, MOST MAGNIFICENT IRONY, YOU HAVE OBTAINED A WEAPON YOU DARE NOT ALLOW BE USED BY ANY NOT OF YOUR OWN BLOOD. FROZEN, CREEPING WHITE SNAKE. HOW COULD YOU RISK GIVING THE HORN INTO THE HANDS OF ONE WHO TRULY IS OF THIS LAND? DO YOU KNOW THE HEARTS OF THOSE YOU RULE? OF THOSE WHO SHOULD BE RULING IN YOUR PLACE? WHO WOULD THE WARRIORS OF FARAK CUT DOWN?**"

Who indeed? Medair stared down at the box. If she used the Horn, would Farak make the final judgment on who deserved death? That was a path Medair had never thought to take, and it seemed to her both right and just. Almost of its own volition, one of her hands lifted.

Cool fingers caught hers.

"There is compulsion in his words," Cor-Ibis murmured, lifting her hand to study tight-strapped bandages. "This is a choice which, if you need to make it, should be made without such." He added a word beneath his breath, the trigger for what must have been a dispell. A cool breeze whisked away the cobwebs tangling Medair's thoughts. She straightened, and looked first at his expressionless face, then at the box.

"MAKE YOUR PEACE WITH YOUR GOD, INELKAR,"
Estarion boomed, and Medair's shoulders tensed. A compulsion in
his words. His prolonged speech to her had more purpose than
demoralising those he was about to fight. She could feel it now that
it struck her afresh, not layered upon her behind the shield of
words.

Cor-Ibis still held her hand, and she dragged her eyes from the
box to his fingers. They glowed faintly, paler even than her
swathing of bandage. The same old arguments trudged a circle in
her mind. Enemy, innocent, oath, trust, betrayal, loss, futility. How
many times did she have to chase the tail of her own internal
rhetoric? She had made her decision.

Momentarily, she tightened her clasp. Cor-Ibis was not Ieskar.
He had never been her enemy. Then she drew her hand free, and
moved away from the Horn, looking inward towards the lights of
the White Palace rather than the fires of the army at the gate. She
would not use the Horn.

"If Farak does not answer, She does not," Medair said, glancing
at the Kier. "But I have never heard that She picks and chooses.
All born to Farakkan are Her children."

"And you, Keris N'Taive?" Kier Inelkar asked the woman who
had been outside the shield when wild magic's Conflagration had
transformed the world and made her into Herald of a kingdom
once thought dust. "What is your judgment?"

"How could it be otherwise?" the Mersian Herald asked, her
eyes shining with sincere faith. "Farak is the mother of all."

Beyond the wall, the whisper had become a chant: steady, full-
throated, accompanied by the tramp of booted feet. The army had
begun to move. They would soon be within bow and spell-shot.

"Casting in the chant, *Ekarrel*," the Keridahl Alar said.

"Massive," Cor-Ibis added. "As if the entire army is
contributing."

"Is it possible? Look to the walls, Antellar."

Protections were always set on the walls of Athere. Over the
day which had just passed, these enchantments had been reinforced
along the southern reaches of Ahrenrhen. Now, at a signal from

Keridahl Antellar, they were strengthened to counteract anything which might be thrown at them in the first advance.

"Now we shall see if the air attack you predicted comes to pass, Keris N'Taive," Keridahl Antellar said. "You are prepared, Cor-Ibis?"

Cor-Ibis inclined his head briefly.

"What of " the Kier began, and everyone looked anxiously at her suddenly arrested stance, head cocked to one side, eyes narrowing. Medair guessed that she was listening to a wend-whisper, a message sent by magic.

"Ekarrel?" asked the Kend, turning from whispering commands to her Das-kend.

"N'Taive, what is the 'Charaine Regiment'?" Kier Inelkar asked.

The Mersian gave the Kier a startled glance which meant she'd asked about something the Herald had assumed she could not *not* know. But wild magic had made the world outside Athere nearly unrecognisable, transforming the loose clans of Mersians into a formidable power, and replacing three kingdoms with an inland sea. A single regiment could have become anything.

"Charaine is the mountainous land to the south of the Forest of the Guardian," N'Taive replied, carefully. "It is where most of your deskai are stationed. The Regiment is a mainstay of Palladium's south-east defences."

"And what are 'deskai'?"

"Deskai..." The Herald shook her head. "There were no deskai in the past where you lived? How horrible!" She made a gesture to acknowledge that now was not the moment to digress. "Vecka, my mount, is part deskai. They are shape-shifters, born to two forms, and to powers more enduring than most mage-cast." She smiled obliquely. "Tanis Araina will find it disconcerting to be forgotten. Deskai are not easily put from the thoughts."

"Your horse can change shape?" asked the Kier, surprised.

"No. Vecka is more horse than deskai. They can breed to either race."

"I see. It would seem this Tanis Araina hurries to our aid. According to her wend-whisper, she is less than a quarter-measure away and regrets her failure to reach us before sunset."

"Wonderful!" exclaimed the Mersian.

Cor-Ibis lifted a hand, a short, sharp movement, adding a few hasty words beneath his breath. The air shuddered, and Medair was nearly knocked from her feet by an invisible blow. She had to clutch the smooth stone of the parapet to keep upright.

"A gate," Cor-Ibis said tersely as the blast died away. Medair's ears were ringing. "Pass on to all points," he ordered Avahn. "If Estarion can produce a gate so soon after transporting his army here, we must focus much of our own defence on counteracting them. Or allow the fight within the walls."

"How can he–?" Avahn asked, then restrained himself, obediently sending messages to mages throughout Athere.

But his question hung in the air, passing in glances between those who waited tensed for the next move. A gate was beyond the strength of even adepts, and could only be produced by melding power in a grouped casting, or through the enhancement of a rahlstone. The use of gates large and enduring enough to transport an army had already warned Athere's defenders that Estarion must have at his command dozens of mages of the highest calibre. That there were enough casters to use gates in battle, in addition to the enchantments which would protect an attacking force from massed sleep or death, suggested immense superiority of both number and strength of casters...as the Palladian Empire's defenders had faced, when the Ibisians had invaded...

"It seems to me," the Kier said into the hush, "that the Horn must be used. If it summons no aid, we have lost nothing. We are outnumbered in a battle where the rules are no longer familiar. I am willing to take the risk that we might hasten our deaths." She signalled one of her attendants to fetch the box.

"In range," the Kend announced, and gave a command which sent a hail of arrows down on the approaching troops. Selected mages added a drift of combative magic – flame darts, poison clouds, blood roses. Medair stepped forward to see the volley hit, and flinched as one of the spells was reflected back to the top of

Ahrenrhen. There was a muffled shriek and a flurry of movement along the wall to the right, where the flame darts had caught a few unprepared. Not so the southern troops, whose raised shields reflected the arrow shot. Most of them hadn't even wavered in their chanting.

Only one of the defenders' spells had not been deflected or dispersed. Medair could see a dull green cloud drifting over the first line of attacker, some distance to the east. But, as she watched, a little whirlwind whipped it away.

With barely a pause, the first two ranks of attackers, all along the vast southern reach of Ahrenrhen, took two running steps forward and launched themselves into the air. Not flying, exactly, but bounding up toward the top of the wall as if they weighed little more than thistledown. Medair backed hastily away as Cor-Ibis snapped out a word of activation.

A blast of icy wind tossed the Southerners awry, and most of them were catapulted backwards to land in the midst of their troops, the upraised swords of their own forces doing more damage than their fall. A few still reached the wall. They were significantly outnumbered, but a giant now stood among Athere's defenders, far along the wall to Medair's right.

Barely had the first wave been flung away when another two ranks of soldiers leapt upwards. Again Cor-Ibis raised a gale sufficient to knock the nearest back, but those further down the wall had not managed it. Medair staggered as Keridahl Antellar disrupted another gate. Cor-Ibis said something about set-spells, but Medair could barely hear him through the ringing in her ears. And then came the song of the Horn, as the Kier opened the box.

Keridahl Antellar warded another gate, but even as those around the Kier's vantage point struggled to remain on their feet, the sky warped and twisted, shimmering as if from the heat of a fire. How could Estarion summon so many, almost more quickly than they could disrupt them?

The gates were drawing vital attention from the army leaping forward, and a surge of new attackers almost gained the wall. Pushing them back meant no-one was able to stop the newest gate, and the sky opened to drop a small cadre of warriors almost at

Medair's elbow. Two silver-clad giants and a dozen soldiers leapt in every direction. The Kier had many protectors, but was only saved from death by a set-spell of her own, which sent the giant lunging for her spinning backwards to land with a thunderous crash on the upward stair. But the attendant standing before her had crumpled to the ground, blood spurting from a gouged throat, and the iron-bound box he carried fell beneath booted feet. The song of the Horn took on a peculiarly ringing note as it clattered into the melee.

Medair, tucked against the inner parapet, found herself facing two women in leather. She choked as an arm wrapped around her throat, and struggled to turn away from her other attacker as she frantically thrust her hand into her satchel.

"The way to the wall's blocked!" one hissed, trying to clap a pad of white cloth impregnated with some noxious substance over Medair's nose.

"Tell me something I don't–" the other began, then shrieked. There was an audible snap as Medair firmly removed the arm about her throat. Smiling, she threw the woman off the wall into the street below. The other went the same way, a moment later.

It felt too good. Medair hastily removed the strength ring, even as she was buffeted by stumbling Ibisians. She didn't dare fight within the curious euphoria of the ring, any more than the Ibisians would risk most of their arsenal of combat spells with enemy and ally in close melee. Invisibility was a far better option and she hastily took it, working to get out of the press of battle. The struggle surged toward the left, where the remaining silver giant was trying to reach the Kier. Medair wriggled in the opposite direction.

Another gate began to form, but someone managed to block it. Medair was knocked from her feet when the Kend – commander of the Ibisian armies – backed into her. All along Ahrenrhen, battles were being won and lost amidst a maelstrom of sound: shouts, rushing wind and the boom of disrupted gates, grunts of pain, a man bellowing, scuffling feet, metal on metal. Close behind her, someone wept. The battle chant of the invaders rose above the cries and small explosions, and winding through it all was the song of the Horn.

From out of the maze of boots skittered the source of that song, followed by two Southerners diving for the prize. Still on her hands and knees, Medair grabbed it reflexively when it struck her chin. As bare flesh touched the bone of a goddess, the power of the Horn filled her and she gasped. It hurt, like running too hard for too long, like a muscle stretched too far, spasming into a knot.

Then one of the Southerners ploughed into her, grabbing for the Horn even as it began to fade into invisibility. If not for the shocking effect of its touch, he probably would have wrested it from her. But he flinched, which gave her the chance to roll away, fetching up against the parapet with the Horn of Farak cradled to her chest. Feet slammed into her back, her leg, and she dragged herself upwards to avoid further injury. The Southerner was searching frantically, unable to pinpoint the source of the song. An opportunistic Atherian spitted him as he struggled toward her.

Something roared, in fury not pain. The giant which had been so determinedly trying to reach the Kier whirled, incidentally cutting down a Southerner and the Keridahl Alar's son. It looked across the heads of the combatants, directly at Medair.

Medair flinched in outright horror as it lunged, pushing aside friend and foe alike. Trapped by the press of battle against the parapet, she scrambled on top of the smooth stone, gripping the Horn by its braided cord. She could see Ileaha at the top of the nearest stair, fighting for her life against two Southerners.

Ileaha. Of two bloods, fiercely loyal to both Palladium and the Kier. There was no more perfect a person to use the Horn. Medair ran unsteadily along the parapet toward her.

Her footing slipped and she gripped a nearby Southerner's shoulder for balance as the air shook from another gate formed, was dispersed, and was almost immediately replaced. There seemed no limit to Estarion's gates. Southern warriors poured into Athere, both onto Ahrenrhen and in the streets below, and the top of the wall became almost impassable, more tightly packed than even the Kier's throne room had been. Medair stopped dead, faced suddenly with three separate silver giants trying to plough their way through a field of flesh towards her.

"Oh, Great Lady!" she groaned aloud.

There was no time. The giant directly ahead of her had reached the inner edge of the wall and was thrusting its way to her position. Several Southerners and Ibisians, having no idea what the giants were chasing, began to turn in the same direction. Whatever the consequences of Medair using the Horn, it was surely better than the artefact falling in the hands of these metal-clad monsters.

Taking a deep breath, Medair clasped the Horn of Farak firmly in flinching hands, and set it to her lips.

he ring which cloaked Medair from sight shattered into dust. That minor hurt was one of the few things she truly felt while the Horn of Farak shook the world. It loosed a clear, beautiful note, high and light, and Medair could well believe they heard it over all Farakkan. As penetrating as the dawn.

Her every fibre, body and soul, resonated with it. She wasn't in pain, not really. She ached, felt as if her heart were being drawn from her breast, but the Horn's power no longer stung her. When it dissolved into light and nothing, she realised she was weeping. The cry of the Horn went on, the single note joined by others, louder and stronger, a chorus which climbed until it seemed impossible that it could scale further heights. Then it stopped.

Into the silence, the stars fell.

"AlKier preserve us!" someone entreated, voice ragged. No-one fought; they had all stopped, enemies standing shoulder to shoulder, waiting to witness Farak's judgment. Even the silver giants were still, helms tilted back to watch the pinpoints of light drop from above. All the mageglows on Ahrenrhen seemed to have been extinguished, and only the fire of the Southerners' weapons still competed with the falling heavens.

Not the stars, after all. They were still there, glinting in the night sky. That which answered the Horn's summons proved to be oval, man-sized. There were tens of thousands of them, falling like snowflakes, a languid drift. The lowest layer halted roughly twelve feet above Medair's position on Ahrenrhen. They were all prisms and facets: sunlight through dew-drops, rainbows on mist, stained glass slowly revolving.

One, dominated by sombre reds and midnight blue, descended lower than its fellows, and came to rest within touching distance of Medair. She stared at it, disarmed by unexpected beauty. Were these the warriors of Farak?

Then the figure changed, a form, a face, becoming visible within the multi-hued glow. Medair's knees gave way, so she almost pitched off the parapet, and was saved by Cor-Ibis, once again trapping her hand in his and pulling her to less chancy ground. Her satchel slipped from her shoulder to tumble to the stair below, but Medair didn't care. She was staring in horror and disbelief at the face of her Emperor.

Of all the possible consequences of using the Horn of Farak, this was the worst. Whether the dead were here to slay Ibisians or Southerners mattered little when weighed against the fact that her Emperor had been dragged from Farak's rest to see the ruins of his Empire. To witness the depth of her betrayal. She bowed her head, unable to meet his bright gaze.

There was no right choice, messenger, said a voice. It did not sound like Grevain Corminevar's. It had more of the Horn in it than any human throat. *And no wrong decision.*

She looked up hastily at the sound of a sword being drawn, and saw that the Emperor had grown more distinct, though he was still formed of nothing more than brilliantly coloured light. The sword was golden, and she had no doubt that it would slice more deeply than any weapon fashioned of base metal. Thousands upon thousands of jewelled warriors followed Grevain Corminevar's lead, raising halberd and spear, sword and bow and dagger. The fire of the Southerners' weapons seemed weak in comparison, and the disparity in numbers was obvious. For every Southern attacker, there were two jewelled spirits hovering in the sky above Athere. It would be an impossibly glorious sight, if only these were not the souls of the dead, come to send others to the grave.

Without further words of either recrimination or absolution, the Emperor turned from Medair. The movement broke the nearest silver giant from its frozen stillness. With a drawn-out cry, the armoured figure swung a great sword stained with blood upward to cut across the spirit's jewelled chest. To no effect.

Medair was barely able to follow the flicker of movement which was the whole of the Emperor's response. The result was much clearer: a precise slash through the silver armour from the centre of its horned helm to the region of its belly. Dark blood spattered as the giant crashed to its knees, and a grey smoke drifted up from the wound. The creature's life essences were boiling on contact with air.

Those nearest in the press atop Ahrenrhen cried out in pain, rubbing frantically at exposed flesh. As the cloud of vapour expanded, Cor-Ibis released another set-spell, still keeping firm hold of Medair. A breeze rose, blasting the vapour away and holding steady. Maintaining such a spell would drain his reserves quickly.

A Southern woman fetched up against Medair either by design or chance. She raised her sword, eyes huge with fear and hatred, but a woman shimmering in milk and turquoise cut her down before she had a chance to strike. Medair stared at the figure which had saved her, then tried to pull away from Cor-Ibis' hold.

"You recognised her?" the Keridahl asked as he fended off a stumbling Atherian. He could well have been seated at his own table, rather than straining to preserve a difficult spell in the midst of battle. His firm clasp of her hand tightened as she attempted to free herself again, then he shifted his hold to her upper arm by way of compromise.

"The Kend," Medair replied, abandoning her attempts to pull away, and ignoring any urge to clutch him in return. "The leader of Kier Ieskar's army, Kend las Rittnar."

His eyes sought the turquoise woman, but the leader of Kier Ieskar's armies was lost among the legion of dead.

"So they fight side by side."

"Dragged from their rest."

Cor-Ibis shook his head, but before he could reply, something at the head of the stair arrested his attention, and the spell-wind vanished. Medair saw that the Kierash, Islantar, had somehow found his way to the battle, and was standing undefended. Cor-Ibis let go of her arm, but before he could move to the heir's side, it became obvious that there was no need. It was over.

The carnage was breath-taking.

Not a single Southerner was left standing on Ahrenrhen, and Medair did not doubt that the thousands who had so recently raised their voice in battle-chant beyond the wall were also lying in pools of their own blood. Medair had never imagined that the Horn would bring such a quick, decisive victory. So terribly one-sided.

She lifted wide, disbelieving eyes to the jewelled spirits. Most were rising slowly into the air. Only one remained, all brilliant red and blue. His bright gaze was fixed on the boy who wore the pale skin of a conqueror, but whose firm jaw revealed his Corminevar heritage.

Heal Palladium, said the Emperor. The ringing, unnatural notes of the Horn made the simple statement an order, a proclamation. It was all he said, before following the army of dead, up away from Athere. They were still beautiful: deadly jewels of light which rose with ever-increasing speed until they were lost among the stars.

๛

Only Cor-Ibis' faint, steady glow remained. He reached out once more and touched Medair's arm. She was not certain if he thought her in need of support, or simply wanted to keep her in reach. Before her eyes could adjust properly to starlight and Keridahl-glow, dozens of magelights were conjured all along the length of Ahrenrhen. The brighter illumination revealed that the stones of the wall were awash with blood. Spirals of noxious vapour continued to rise from the bodies of the fallen giants, and those nearest the fumes were the first to move, picking their way awkwardly across the corpses of enemies and allies.

"So *many*," someone said.

"An army able to defeat any other." The Kier, after a lingering glance at her son, crossed the slick stone to where Medair stood. "A more decisive battle than any could have expected. Again, Keris an Rynstar, I can only offer you my gratitude."

Medair just turned away. Unforgivably rude, but she could not face this woman's thanks or the reason for them. She could not do anything but struggle to remain upright, for if she fell she would be kneeling in the blood of those for whom she had summoned death. She could smell it. The air was full of a thick iron tang, wet with it.

The Ibisians allowed her to stand alone, gazing up at the palace. She wanted to shut out their voices as well, but that was not so easy.

"We must stop these fumes," said a voice she didn't know, and someone began to cast, voice muted. No more set-spells ready, it seemed, and no doubt reserves were low. The battle had so nearly gone the other way. Outnumbered and for once magically outmatched, the Ibisians would have crumbled and fallen under the onslaught. Burning swords inside the walls, Palladian White Snake blood running in the streets. Instead, Athere had lost a few hundred at most, and an entire army was dead. Because Medair had blown the Horn.

They were discussing funeral pyres behind her; ways to efficiently dispose of bodies. The corpses of men and women, of the army of Decians who had come to retake an Empire, and overthrow a thief. The conversation had an air of unreality, and more than one voice shook. Even Ibisians could not quite hide the horror that any sane person must feel at having witnessed death. Or perhaps they merely trembled at thoughts of their narrow escape, after they had been so nearly overwhelmed.

What had Estarion said? "A name of hope and honour. A name which made a promise." This was what she had set out to do, after all: defend Athere from invasion. Everything had changed, yet was still the same. But as with every decision Medair had made, she was left with a heavy load of consequence and hurt. She had used the Horn and thousands had died and she was not even certain it made any difference. Not to the deep, festering wound at the heart of an invaded land.

A familiar brown leather shape was pushed into her hands.

"I think you dropped this," Avahn said. He waited until her fingers had closed on the satchel before letting go. Medair looked down at the symbol of a role she could no longer claim as her own. Could she do nothing but betray the past? The Horn had drawn Medair's own people back from the dead to fight beside Ibisians, to save Ibisians. No right choice, no wrong decision. That didn't make it any better.

"There are some Southerners still alive," Avahn told her. "Among the wounded. And there are even small groups untouched outside the walls. It seems that if they dropped their weapons they were spared, though few enough did that. The smart ones are fleeing, but they'll be rounded up soon enough."

He paused, perhaps waiting for a response, but Medair had gone to a place beyond words, where there was only blood, and her name.

"Riders to the east!" someone exclaimed sharply.

Avahn must be using a night-sight enchantment, since he seemed able to see through the gloom, peering into the distance. "Not 'riders', I should think," he murmured. "Keris N'Taive called them 'deskai', didn't she? This, I want to see." He turned back to Medair. "Come down with me when the Kier greets these marvellous vassals for the first time. Else I will not be able to witness it."

"You've been given the job of looking after me," Medair said. Her voice was small, a thread.

"Just so. Come down, Medair. Refusal is not an option."

Resistance, at least, was too much effort. Medair allowed him to guide her down the stair and out Aerele Gate, all the time aware of walking through the blood of the people she had killed, stepping over outflung arms. Only the gloom made it possible to pass, hiding the faces of the men and women whose lives had been taken by the Horn.

There was a patch of clear grass, close enough to the Kier to listen, and reaching it Medair refused to go further. As more magelights were summoned she stared into the dark to have something to look at which was neither the Ibisians she had saved, nor the Farakkians lying still and bloody.

Those who approached were not riders, but a small army of riderless horses, most black or dark brown. As the main body slowed, a distinctive pale grey horse led a small detachment forward to the city. Each and every one of them trotted at least a foot above the ground, a fortunate thing considering the thousands of corpses.

Although the deskai bore no saddles or bridles, each of them had an odd arrangement of cloth and leather slung around their necks. The purpose of this burden became clear after the lead group had halted some thirty feet from the gate. They underwent a swift, writhing twist which was less than pleasant to watch and suddenly there were nine men and women instead. All were well over seven feet tall. Each made identical movements to tie apron-like garments around their not-inconsiderable waists. Their skin ranged from pink-pale to charcoal darker even than the people of the Farakkan's south-west.

The grey had turned into a dark young woman with short-cropped white hair. Tanis Araina, Medair presumed.

"*Ekarrel.*" The deskai leader was smiling in open relief as she executed a precise bow. "Praise to the Four, you are unharmed!"

"My thanks, Keris Araina," the Kier said. Nothing in Inelkar's face betrayed that she had not met this woman before. But Keris Araina's entire race hadn't existed a day ago, and the Kier must be wondering what to say to her. This was now no more Inelkar's world than it was Medair's.

A touch on her arm drew her attention and she found the Kierash, under Cor-Ibis' escort, at her shoulder.

"Keris an Rynstar," the boy began. "I recognise that now is not the time, but I would like to speak with you, at your convenience."

Medair's lips curved, though she doubted it was a cheerful expression. She needed only one more push to shame herself with hysteria.

"There's so little to say, Kierash." She lifted one booted foot, drawing attention to the blood-grimed soles. "Would you ask me of Decia? Of the south I knew, so staunchly prepared to support the Emperor in war? Those Decians, Duchess Trienne, considered it a proud thing to die in battle for a cause in which they believed. Where is the pride in being cut down by an enemy you cannot wound? Do you want me to try and guess whether they felt their cause was just?" She had to stop, or she would shout at him.

"That is something I will do on my own," Islantar replied, with a gravity Medair would have thought unnatural in any Farakkian youth. "I would ask you of them, though. The Decians you knew, so different from those we deal with today. And the Ibis-lar you knew, who brought down the Empire. If I am–" For the first time the boy hesitated, pale lashes dropping. "If I am to heal the present, I must know the past."

"You will need more than knowledge for that," Medair said.

"Yes."

It was simple agreement. Islantar, raised to rule, probably had a better grasp of the problems he faced than she did. The question of what came next, of how thousands of dead Decians could possibly help ease long-nurtured hatred, hung between them. There was a long pause.

Cor-Ibis moved a hand sharply, and the air shook with a sudden concussion.

"Another gate?" Avahn turned, then his eyes went wide and disbelieving and he made a similar fending gesture. "But who?"

The Keridahl didn't answer as the air about them thrummed, threatening to knock them from their feet. Some of the deskai began to run toward Medair's location. A woman nearer to the wall shouted and even Islantar joined the effort to stave off gate after gate. The air blurred and seemed to twist. The scent of hot metal drowned out the stench of blood.

And then it was too much. Avahn stumbled. Bright light washed over them, then darkness, and Medair felt abruptly weightless. The ground shifted.

FOUR

edair, on her hands and knees, found leaves and dirt beneath her palms. Her eyes struggled to adjust to the sudden absence of warm magelight, and in the aftermath of so many disrupted gates she was slow to process the sounds of surprise and distress. Forcing herself to unsteady feet, she fetched up against rough bark. A tree, where one had not been. Or, rather, she was no longer outside the walls of Athere, where the flat swathe of grass was covered in blood and bodies. Instead, the moon peeped through a thick canopy of leaves. There was a steady murmur of magic, and a stiff, cold breeze carried the scent of wood smoke. The knees of her trousers were damp and a drop of icy water scored her cheek. It had been raining.

"Where are we?" It was Ileaha's voice, as startled as Medair felt.

"Don't summon a light," Cor-Ibis said. "Not until we know where this is."

This coming from a man who, as their eyes adjusted to the darkness, proved to still be glowing steadily. After a pause, the Keridahl continued. "Who is here?"

"I am," said Kierash Islantar, just the tiniest note of uncertainty in his voice. Someone inhaled and even Medair felt a twinge of dismay to know that Palladium's heir had been stolen away to wherever this was. He was so close Medair edged almost automatically away, then stopped, staring up through a break in the canopy.

"And I," said N'Taive, the Herald of the Mersians. Medair had not seen her among the small group trailing Cor-Ibis and the Kierash, but she recognised the lilt of her voice.

"At your command, Keridahl," said Liak ar Haedrin, at the same time as Avahn's quiet: "Here."

"Kaschens las Cormar and an Serentel," said the voice of a stranger, confident and female.

"At your command," concluded a young man, presumably Kaschen an Serentel. The gate had evidently scooped up a couple of soldiers.

There was a pause, and Medair knew they waited for her to speak. She felt so remote from them, from everything. She had admitted her name, she had used the Horn, and become an unspeakable thing, drenched in blood. What was there left for her?

But remaining silent was no longer an option.

"I am here," she said, close to whispering. "Here in Decia, if that truly is Castle Gyrfalcon."

Through the trees she could see a jagged hill, a sharply vertical mound of ragged stone and rubble surmounted by weirdly glistening black stone. A dark castle whose myriad windows were outlined by an orange glow. The shape of it was very like the castle where Duchess Trienne had received her so graciously. Yet this was the stuff of nightmares: grim, unwelcoming and sinister.

"Falcon Black!" The Mersian Herald's voice was stiff with dismay.

"Decia, but not imprisoned," Avahn said, rapidly reviewing the situation. "Why did those summoned by the Horn spare Estarion? And why, after sending us through a gate to Decia, did he leave us outside the castle and unguarded?"

"The forests around Falcon Black are bewitched," Herald N'Taive said. Her voice, once so stalwart, quavered. "Haunted, spelled, trapped. No army dare approach the Cloaked South's stronghold."

"Even so, to leave us loose..."

"Possibly the many gates we disrupted skewed the one which succeeded," suggested Islantar. The Kierash had recovered his equanimity, his voice steady.

"Sending us to the moat instead of the dungeon?" Cor-Ibis did not seem convinced, but he moved on briskly. "Only a supremely powerful artefact could have produced so many gates, and they are not always predictable. Whatever the case, we are in unfamiliar territory, and our very appearance proclaims us enemy. Avahn, Kel ar Haedrin, you will protect the Kierash. Keris N'Taive, if this forest is trapped, we need to know as much as you can tell us about it, and quickly."

"Of course." Herald N'Taive regained a little of her composure. "My Queen sent me here several times, before Estarion broke the Compact. To the south there is farmland and Taedrin City is not far to the east. North and west, as well as immediately around the castle, is forest with a single road east, heavily guarded. The last time I was at Falcon Black, there were wild stories that Estarion had started hunting criminals through the western forest. More challenging sport than his usual fare. It was true. It pleased him to take me as witness–" Her voice wavered.

"I have not seen Falcon Black from this angle, so I can only guess that this is the northern forest, which is denser, and forbidden to everyone. A shield against invasion from the north. It is said that the enchantments which protect the forest directly about the castle extend into the northern reaches."

Medair shifted uneasily. It was as if the Mersian Herald didn't want to describe the dangers of the forest exactly, for fear of summoning them up.

"It has been a long time since any army approached from the north, not for fifty years or more. There were few survivors from the attempt. They spoke of losing their companions because of poor weather, and of something which snatched the soldiers, one by one, before they even came within sight of Falcon Black."

"What of smaller groups? An army is a large target." Cor-Ibis sounded distracted. The glow which emanated from him was not powerful, just enough to make him visible, and she could not make out his expression as he turned his head to look up towards the castle.

"Of those known to have dared in the last ten years, only one has returned. Five months after setting out, haggard, gravely injured and not remembering a moment after he ventured into the forest."

"Then the road's the safer way out," Avahn said, thoughtful but undaunted. "It might be guarded, but it's better than trying to head north when it's obvious Decia has set powerful defences."

"Won't those defences be more concentrated about the castle?" Ileaha asked.

"Very likely," Cor-Ibis said. "I agree that the risk must be less than venturing through this forest. East to the castle's entrance – the point where the road begins to ascend. We can hope that such a well-frequented place will prove to be less deadly."

"And beyond that point? A well-guarded road is not so easy to pass as a set-spell whose trigger you can detect and avoid." Cor-Ibis' glimmering form was briefly eclipsed as Avahn moved towards him. "And past the road? We are in Decia."

"The road must wait until daylight, at the very least," Cor-Ibis agreed.

"And I know of one who will aid us, in Taedrin City," offered Herald N'Taive. "If we can reach her, we have shelter, resources."

"Is it at all viable to build our own gate, Illukar?" Avahn asked.

"Between us, when we have recovered, we could do that. I have a rahlstone, though it must be nearing the limits of its use. However, it is unlikely that we could complete a gate before being set upon, and we cannot even make an attempt tonight, nor, I fear, tomorrow. Too much of our strength has been spent in battle. Until then, we need shelter, a defensible position and more information with which to plan our next move. Fortunately, we are not all obviously Palladian."

"And Estarion?" the Kierash asked, speaking after a long silence. "Estarion, who is mad enough to summon wild magic when his plans for victory go awry? Estarion who we believe holds an artefact capable of summoning gates of unlimited power and frequency?"

"And who may be hunting us as we speak," Cor-Ibis finished, composure steady in the face of so many obstacles. "I have not overlooked his threat, but I wish to see the road first. If its guards are easily avoided – as they may be, when Decia's forces are surely in disarray following the mass departure to war – then I will be able to send you on to Taedrin City while I attempt Estarion. But your safety must come first, Kierash."

"Palladium must come first, Keridahl," Islantar said, stiffly. "We cannot turn aside from Estarion's threat, not even if it were my mother's life at risk."

"Perhaps." Cor-Ibis' tone suggested that Islantar would be sent to safety no matter what his objections. "In either case, our first move must be to shelter."

"Falcon Hill is pocked with a maze of caves and caverns," N'Taive suggested. "I saw dozens of entrances on my previous visits. Estarion is rumoured to have chambers within, and I know that one entrance is guarded, near the top of the road. I would not care to venture deeply into any of them, but there are enough shallow depressions to at least get us out of this damp."

"Where we can discuss this further," Cor-Ibis said. "And, if you will agree to it, Keris an Rynstar, to examine the rest of the Hoard of Kersym Bleak."

"The rest—?" Avahn repeated.

"I took away more than the Horn, Avahn," Medair replied. She knew Cor-Ibis well enough to have expected that he would stop ignoring the implications of the 'hoard' linked to the legend of the Horn when the situation required it.

"Of course." Avahn's voice was rich with self-disgust. "Well, I'll beat myself over the head about that later. Shall we get on?"

"Close together," Kel ar Haedrin suggested. "And slowly."

They moved towards the understated beacon provided by Cor-Ibis and it seemed to Medair that she had taken no more than two steps when the pulse of magic so densely present in the forest altered.

"It's reacting to us," Cor-Ibis said. "Be alert for anything."

"Mist," said one of the kaschens, the no-longer confident female. It closed around them with startling speed, a dense cloud rising from the ground, curling and twisting in the wind.

"Clasp hands," Cor-Ibis said, his voice as muffled as a man speaking from beneath ten blankets. Medair thought he said something further, but could not make it out. The mist closed around her like a cage.

Reaching out, she tried to find Islantar, who had been closest, but her fingers touched only icy vapour.

"Hello?" she said, then repeated herself, more loudly. Her voice sounded distant to her own ears, and she could hear nothing from those who had been only a few feet away moments before. She was alone in a still and silent world of white, the wind cut off as completely as the Keridahl.

෨ව

Being literally muffled made Medair feel far less detached from the question of present and future. Resisting a panicky impulse to run forward groping for her companions, she stood still, attempting to orient herself. She had been facing Gyrfalcon Castle – or Falcon Black, as Herald N'Taive called it. If she could somehow continue in a straight line, she should find her way to the hill's base.

Spreading her arms wide in the hopes of encountering the others as she moved, Medair took two steps forward. Her right fingers brushed something and she gasped, but it was only the bark of another tree. It was fortunate that Falcon Hill was a large target, as she doubted that she could keep to a straight line through thick forest. She could only hope to head in the same general direction until she found something other than trees and mist.

Concentrating on keeping to a straight line, Medair walked directly into someone's back, merely a dim shape through the shrouding mist. Her heart leapt in fright, even though she knew it had to be one of her companions. A face came close to hers, the outline barely recognizable as Avahn.

"Medair," he said, voice muted even at close range. A shape loomed at his shoulder, easily identifiable by the faint luminescence which clung to him. They formed a loose triangle, both Cor-Ibis men taking one of her arms, as if the mist might snatch her away.

"You were closest to Kierash Islantar, Keris," said Cor-Ibis. His clasp on her wrist seemed unnecessarily firm. "Can we hope to retrace your steps?" he continued, and she took reassurance from his businesslike tone.

"He was directly before me," she replied, shaking her head uselessly in the gloom. "I walked through the place he had been standing and there was no-one in reach."

"The mist disorients as well as obscures," Cor-Ibis said. At close quarters, the glow of his skin clearly revealed his drawn face. Had he rested after the enormity of the shield-casting? The set-spells he'd cast on the wall could have been prepared over the last handful days, but more likely only in the previous few hours. And then he'd released them in rapid succession, each instance an additional drain on his reserves. They were in the heart of Decia, and he had none of the advantages of his adept's strength.

Nor did he quite retain his usual calm, not with Palladium's heir brought to the enemy's stronghold. "The Kierash could be two feet from us and we would not know. A dispell may help, but I doubt it could vanquish this mist."

"If it cleared a small area, we will at least be able to collect any others, like Medair, who have not travelled far."

"Avahn, are you as close to having exhausted your reserves as your cousin?" Medair asked, trying to make out his face in the tiny amount of light Cor-Ibis emanated.

"Not quite." She thought he smiled. "It's not often I can expect my casting to be more powerful than yours, Illukar."

"Just do not overestimate your reserve," Cor-Ibis replied, looking about them as the mist seemed to close more tightly, filaments of white threading through strands of hair escaping his once neat plait. "If you do not have another set, cast quickly, before they move on."

Avahn nodded, releasing Medair's arm but staying so close his elbow brushed her as he made rapid passes. A dispell did not take long to cast, but every moment gave the others the chance to move out of range. While Avahn worked, Cor-Ibis cast a set spell mageglow, which gave the cloaking mist a warm glow but by no means cut through it.

A rush of air accompanied the activation of Avahn's dispell, and they found themselves at the centre of a large dome beneath the mist. Standing at the very edge, in the direction Medair was facing, was the Mersian Herald. She held an arm protruding from the mist and Medair felt Cor-Ibis' grip on her own arm tighten as N'Taive pulled a young Ibisian woman dressed in the uniform of a kaschen into the clearing. There was no trace of Islantar, Ileaha, Kel ar Haedrin or the other kaschen.

"Do you have rope?" Cor-Ibis asked, already moving beyond his disappointment to practicalities. His voice seemed loud in the absence of the mist.

Medair nodded, and opened her satchel. Avahn crossed the clearing to take a firm grip on the Mersian, scanning the edges of the mist as he went for any more disembodied limbs. Then the dome collapsed, instantly cutting Medair and Cor-Ibis off from Avahn and the two women.

After a moment's complete stillness, Cor-Ibis took the rope Medair had pulled too late from her satchel, coiled it first about his own waist, then bound a triple loop about Medair.

"Could you cast another dispell?" she asked.

"I could, yes. But I will not risk spell shock at this juncture. Avahn will take them to the castle and, if the AlKier is with us, we will be able to meet near the road after this mist lifts."

"If any of them still have their bearings," she pointed out as he took her hand.

"The castle is heavy with power," he said. "More than enough for Avahn or Islantar to detect, even through the hazing effect of this forest's enchantments. Kel ar Haedrin, the other soldier and Ileaha, however, will need a great deal of luck." He started forward slowly.

Medair was certain that she would remember this short journey as the worst in her life. Falcon Black had not been far away, but pushing blindly through a dense wood on a cold, damp night was a nightmarish experience, exacerbated by the cottony silence which buried even the rustle of fallen leaves beneath their feet. It made her feel impossibly alone, reminding her endlessly of the world which had been twice cut away from her.

The rope binding her to Cor-Ibis did not help: snagging on bushes and branches. At one time it stopped them in their tracks as it caught firmly on some invisible obstruction. Medair prayed silently to Farak to guide Ileaha and the others safely and tried not to think of the obstacles which lay ahead of them, even if they could reunite.

Clear air.

Medair let out her breath, barely suppressing a cry at the suddenness of the change. Cor-Ibis had brought them to a corridor between the steep, jagged base of Falcon Hill and the smothered forest. The mist formed an improbable wall, only a few tendrils venturing into the open space. The moon, high in the sky, lit the corridor like a festival light.

After endless blind stumbling, Medair found the sudden transition wholly disorienting. The sharp wind cut through her clothes while barely stirring the white wall from which they had emerged. The back of her neck ached with tension, and she took slow, steady breaths to try and quell her shaking.

Cor-Ibis dismissed his mageglow, then produced a swatch of cloth from within his demi-robe. Dabbing at a bleeding scratch which stretched from the corner of his eye down his cheek, he surveyed their surroundings. Medair had not fared as badly, though her hands were marked with tiny slashes and there was a painful welt on the side of her throat. She was cold and damp, with no hope of a hot bath or warm bed in the near future.

Cold, at least, she could try to do something about. She fished a thick jacket from her satchel and then her lambs wool cloak for Cor-Ibis, who donned it without comment.

"Should we wait for the others?" she asked, her voice sounding loud and unfamiliar to numbed ears. She started to untwist the rope about her waist.

"No. Even if we could be sure they had not reached this point before us, this is too exposed." He was gazing upwards to towers and walkways, then noticed her untying the rope and held out a deterring hand. "We may need to retreat to the mist, if there are patrols or watchers."

They had barely started circling east when they discovered the first cave, the opening nearly ten paces across and twice Medair's height. A gate of dull black metal blocked the way, and Medair could see little in the inky blackness beyond the bars. Then she heard something move within, and backed away. The gate appeared to be designed to raise up into the rock and there was a faint scent of animal, not wholly unpleasant.

"Something which snatches," Cor-Ibis suggested. "Whoever is meant to raise the gates when the mist descends has not been attending his duty."

Medair stared at his cool profile, then continued walking. She felt a brief resistance on the rope before he too moved away from the cave.

"Had you been in Decia, before the Conflagration?" she asked, turning her mind from the ordeal she had just endured and whatever was within that cage. There were too many things she couldn't bear thinking of.

"Not officially."

More shape-changing. "Was it as...foul?"

"No. Estarion was simply a greedy man. Competitive, domineering, but not cruel. A capable leader, although he left much of the practicalities of his rule to his sister, preferring to treat and deal and scheme for expansion. He had a hatred of losing, for it rocked his belief in his own superiority. It is not altogether surprising that he was arrogant enough to turn to wild magic, though I might wish I had anticipated it."

"Why would he remake Decia into *this?*" she asked, staring up. The castle was like the backdrop to a mummer's play: lowering, evil, and wrong.

"I doubt he had any thought of transformation. Certainly no considered scheme of any would-be conqueror need include the resurrection of the Mersians' capital, or the creation of inland seas – or gods. Estarion merely opened a door."

"If he does so again, what determines if there'll be another Conflagration, or the creeping blackness which took Sar-Ibis?"

He didn't answer, looking ahead at another cave closed off with an iron gate.

"This is different," Medair said, stopping some distance from the gate and wrinkling her nose at the rank scent. A high, whining growl whipped into the night, redolent with hunger and frustration, and Medair was hard put not to step back. "Not what was in the last cave."

"No. I do not recognise the cry, but this is obviously a predator. The last cage was not a meat-eater, unless I miss my guess. Perhaps food for this one, or for some other purpose." He took her arm and they edged past the cave, then several more without gates as they made their way around to the eastern face of Falcon Hill.

A ramp stretched down from the southern corner of the hill toward the road east. Medair and Cor-Ibis, at the northern corner, were able to gaze directly along the ascent as it rose through two blockhouses to the massive castle gates. Great braziers on either side of the gates held tapering mounds of fire, reminding Medair inevitably of the Conflagration. Orange light gleamed off brass bindings. Both of the blockhouses were also alight, huge bowls of leaping fire on the flat roofs of the watching posts, casting the heavy portcullises below into deep shadow.

"The road east is likely also blocked," Cor-Ibis said. "When the moon drops the shadow of the hill would shield us most of the way to the first fortification, but we will not risk going so close. That rock bluff three-quarters of the distance along is ideal, for we will need to cross unseen in the morning."

"Through the forest again?"

"That remains to be seen. We will need to keep to the edge of the mist along here."

That was hard, to step back into the muffling chill, and walk almost wholly submerged. The corridor, clear of both mist and trees, drew her toward exposure, but though the watching-posts were distant, whoever manned them would surely have been alerted by the rise of the mist. Anyone striding along the gap would be asking for notice.

Before reaching the spur, Cor-Ibis stopped again.

"Can you climb this?" he asked, gazing across the corridor to the shadowy rocks rising upward.

The hill was not a sheer wall, closer to ladder than slope, but the sharp-cut moonlight created inky shadows which would make footing more than uncertain. "Probably," she said, touching the rope which bound them. His faint glow was nothing in the mist, or even the corridor, but would stand out against the black and silver of the rocks.

She tried to make out what it was he was looking at, and thought she could see a darker outline directly above. The prospect of finding a place to shelter for the night did not cheer her, not when she would be alone with Cor-Ibis.

Before heading up, they took advantage of the muffling quality of the mist to relieve themselves, then Medair coiled the rope and tucked it back into her satchel. The ascent proved relatively easy, though Medair's shins gained several bruises in the process because they could not risk going slowly.

Keridahl-glow did little to help Medair navigate the cave entrance, which gave them room to move side by side, but not quite enough for Cor-Ibis to stand upright. He motioned for her to wait, and felt his way blindly forward, head lowered. She could see from the way he bent further that they had not found anything sizeable.

"The base is almost level," he said, returning, "but it lowers and narrows, and I believe ends shortly beyond the point I could reach." He glanced at a spike of rock on the ramp side of the cave's entrance, which cut off view of the watching-posts. "We will wait here for dawn."

Medair turned to practicalities, because there were an overwhelming number of things she did not want to think about. They could not stand comfortably in the cave, and the fact that Cor-Ibis had not cast a simple night-sight enchantment told her how very near the edge of exhaustion he was. She groped in her satchel, knowing she would have to stand guard while he rested.

Bedrolls and blankets served to pad the uneven floor, and they sat on the rim of the cave entrance to eat the modest meal fished from the depths of Medair's satchel. Dried fruit, nuts and stale biscuits. But now that they were out of the wind, and were no longer focused on moving, black memory threatened to crush her. The weight of it was exhausting. How long had it been, since she had woken? She'd lost track of time after the Horn.

"Do you want to go through Bleak's Hoard tonight?" she asked, searching for some useful occupation.

"Describe it to me."

Medair made a soft noise in her throat. No small task. "There are twelve rings," she said. "No, eleven now, since the invisibility one shattered. One gives strength, along with recklessness. One controls animals – much in the manner of the *vellin* spell. One teleports the wearer to a place within sight. I haven't the sensitivity for divination, so the others remain unknown, just as I don't know the function of four bracelets, seven swords, twelve knives, sixteen amulets, and a necklace and crown which appear to be part of a set. There's a shield-caster which will cover, oh, a circle four feet in diameter. Dozens of small objects – a set of cards, tiny scales, statuettes – which I never even attempted to understand. The necklace and crown, one of the swords and a statuette are all so extraordinarily powerful that I wouldn't suggest even taking them from my satchel. Any strong mage in the castle would sense them, for they proclaim their power almost as loudly as the Horn."

"Divination would best be left for the morning," Cor-Ibis said. If he was surprised at how little she knew about the Hoard, he didn't reveal it. "When our minds are clearer and it is possible to see without attracting attention with mageglows." He lifted one faintly shining hand, perhaps ironically. "Do you have strength enough to cast wend-whispers, Keris? We can try to coordinate rejoining in the morning, though it will not be a simple matter, particularly if the mist rises again."

"To Avahn and Ileaha, yes. The Kierash, perhaps the Mersian, I will try." While not a complex spell, a wend-whisper required an exact mental impression to mark the recipient.

They settled the wording of a brief message, and Medair lost herself to the precision of casting. It was worth an attempt, though there was no guarantee the bubbles of words she was creating would reach even Avahn and Ileaha. Wend-whispers were described as 'relentless butterflies': they would keep on until they found their goal, but their course might be far from linear, and any careless foot could crush them. With their missing companions so close by chances should be high, but the cloaking mist would be poorly designed if it did not interfere with exactly this sort of communication.

"Could you cast a trace, if we can't find them?" she asked, when the last of the messages blundered into the night.

"I might, with some difficulty, establish a link to those most familiar to me without having some object of theirs to focus upon. The chances of failure are high."

Medair stiffened. He had lifted his hands, and his fingers brushed her collarbone, her throat, then found the cord of the invested spell she wore.

"You have worn this long enough that I could use it to trace you if we are separated," he said, lifting it over her head. "My chances certainly increase when you are not wearing it."

He slid the ward into his robe. Then, after the most minute of pauses, reached out and took her hands in his.

FIVE

on't."

It was a feeble protest, and his long fingers only shifted a fraction in response. He was silent and she couldn't say anything more, knowing how much she needed to pull away, and completely incapable of making that tiny, tremendous effort. They sat there, hand-in-hand at the mouth of the cave, while futility chased its tail around Medair's mind.

She had admitted some of her feelings to herself, but to do anything about them was impossible. He would never stop being Ibisian and she would always be Medair an Rynstar. Loyal Palladian, failed hero. Butcher.

"Do you remember our last meeting before the Conflagration?"

"Y-yes," she said, uncertainly. That had been on the balcony, when he had theorised about her past.

"I have never regretted a moment more than that," he said. His voice was as soft and calm as ever, and so bare in its sincerity that she had to stop herself from flinching.

"I knew that my people had given you reason to hate," he went on, choosing his words with eggshell care. "I know now that to you I am a man who might be Palladian but is foremost a White Snake, one of the people who brought down the Empire you served. I am everything you should hate, and if you do not, you will feel in your heart that you have turned your face from all you failed to save."

He glanced at her, and she couldn't say anything, because he had put her feelings into words exactly.

"That night, I wanted to tell you that nothing would please me more than to name you mine, to have between us a certainty which banished distance. And I did not. I thought it too cruel. It is my eternal fortune to be allowed to make that choice again and, though the moment is perhaps harsher still, this time I do not bow down to the hold of the past."

"I am the past," she said, finally gathering the will to pull her hands from his, but his fingers tightened and held her still.

"You are from the past," he said, firmly. "I doubt I will ever succeed in freeing you completely from that cage, from the weight of circumstance crushing you. But you are not failing the dead by living, Medair. You are here, now, and I would be–" He stopped and she heard him take a breath; the imperturbable Illukar, struggling for words.

The thousand arguments she needed to fling in his face would not come to her, sabotaged by a pathetic need.

He looked down, then traced a question on her palm. "Even without your past, we did not have an auspicious start," he said, and she was again conscious of the excruciating care with which he spoke. "A geas by way of introduction and spell-shock to exacerbate matters. You had so many reasons to be angry, and you did not quite hide that there was an old enmity to spice the mix. And you were so meticulously, so scrupulously just. When every feeling must have urged you against it, you returned the rahlstones to me. Purely because you believed it the right thing to do. I have rarely met such honour." He paused again, then raised his head. "I have loved you from that moment," he said, and his voice was raw.

Out of sheer, numb-minded stupidity she tightened her hands in his and that was sufficient encouragement for him to lean forward, to touch her lips with his. His skin was cool and he kissed her with exquisite care, all Ibisian delicacy, but the quiver which ran through his hands matched her own.

Her throat tightened with panic, and she broke away. "I can't do this," she said, but she had to force the words, to not shout her need for him. He remained very still for a moment, then drew back as well, though not nearly far enough for her peace of mind.

"Hardly the place, I know," he said, and his voice was fully mastered once again. There was a time she had thought Ibisians a wholly passionless race, but their extreme control was no indication of their hearts.

"I'm sorry," she said, and felt foolish.

"Now tell me why," he said, as merciless as Ieskar. And not nearly so dead.

She choked on arguments which ran in every direction.

"If I had spoken, the night of the Conflagration, I would not have been able to sway you," he went on, thoughtfully. His calm had returned, perhaps bolstered by her obvious confusion. She should not have leaned into his embrace, should not have pressed against him as if she'd been waiting an eternity to do so.

She should be able to not hate the idea of loving him.

"You still had the Horn then, and all your secrets," he continued. "Your oath to the throne, your office as Herald, and the legend built up about your name. But now everything has changed. You proclaimed yourself before Kier Inelkar. You left your badge of office on the floor of the throne room. You used the Horn to defend Athere and fulfilled the legend in doing so. There is no bar left, no true reason. Not the sheer simple fact of my race."

Battered by all she had done that day, Medair shuddered. She did not feel freed by her use of the Horn, but further trapped in a succession of wrongs which could not be righted.

"No legend involved slaughtering people who thought themselves loyal to Palladium," she said harshly, and realised with a plummeting disgust that she was hoping that he would convince her, that he would reason a way out of the endless loop of rhetoric in her head. That she could allow herself to believe that she had done only what was necessary, and that it was right to stop hating.

"You heard the words of your Emperor," he said. "There was no thread of blame. You heard his words to the Kierash. Your oath is to Palladium, Islantar is its future. There is no conflict, no–" He stopped, perhaps sensing that part of her was stubbornly attempting to close her mind to any hope of a future. That part of her calling him White Snake still, even blaming him for what she had needed to do.

Then those cool, slim fingers touched her cheek and he spoke in a whisper which did not hide how very afraid he was. "Please, Medair."

He took a breath to continue, but did not, turning his head attentively. Medair, so close, caught a faint shred of sound but could not make it out.

"A wend-whisper?" she asked, unspeakably relieved by the interruption.

"The Kierash." Cor-Ibis had straightened, and was surveying the forest below. "He has found a large cave, in the shadow of that spur of rock. I will bring him back here. Better to have him high, if any of those animals are released."

"No." Medair held out a belaying hand, but stopped short of touching him. "I'll go. Unless you can dim that glow, it's too great a risk for you to cross those shadows twice more."

She didn't give him a chance to argue, slipping her satchel from her shoulder and plunging down the slope, by some fortune managing it without more than a knocked elbow. She crossed the passage into the mist without hesitation, and then stopped dead, folding over.

What had she been doing? What did Cor-Ibis think they could do? Impossible. To touch, to talk of love, after she had stood on the walls of Athere and summoned death.

He had known she might run from him, from her response to him. That was why he had taken her trace ward. Part of Medair wanted to do exactly that, to keep walking into the mist, to get as much distance between them as possible, so she could never again hear him say 'please'. But, if she ran at all, it could not be now. There would be time enough later for cowardice.

Taking a deep breath, Medair turned, walking along the border of the mist, near enough to stir the edge's tendrils for a few steps before sinking back. Her link to her satchel made it easy to keep track of the cave where Cor-Ibis waited, so her only difficulty in reaching the spur of rock was the uneven ground and the occasional bush or branch.

A single step took her into the spur's shadow, and she followed its shape with her hand as she moved out of moonglow into pitch.

"Keris."

Kierash Islantar, nowhere near as drained as Cor-Ibis, had obviously cast a night-sight enchantment. A step in the dark and he was with her, this boy the Emperor had commanded to heal Palladium. While it might not be possible for Medair to find a right way forward, she could at least support those words. Ibisian blood

51

or not, this was Palladium's heir, and the only thing she could see to do was get him safely out of Decia.

"I am glad to discover you safe, Keris," he said, formal as ever.

"Can any of us be safe here?" she asked. "The Keridahl has at least found a more sheltered cave."

She turned, less than willing to talk, and he followed her obediently across to the mist. Without the rope, she thought it best to take his hand, and led him with only a few stumbles to the point below the cave. From that angle, Cor-Ibis' glow could be mistaken for a reflection of moonlight, and was not the beacon she had feared. So long as he stayed still, it was unlikely to lead any Decians to them.

"Follow close," she murmured to Islantar, and led him quickly up to join that still, gleaming figure.

"Kierash."

"Keridahl." For a moment Islantar's youth showed in a tone of simple relief, then he moved forward, kneeling as he discovered the low ceiling. "Where did you find these blankets?" he asked. "Ah, of course. Your satchel, Keris, is a wonder beyond compare."

"I–" Hearing the quaver in her voice, Medair made an effort to pull herself together. She would go mad while this habit of hatred struggled against its opposite. "I can offer you a meal of sorts, Kierash," she said, almost steadily. "Dried fruit, nuts, even brandy."

She also produced a spare jacket, and more blankets. They were manoeuvring around the problem of three people sitting in a cave barely able to accommodate them when a cry rose above the muffled silence of the fog. A scream, eldritch and unnatural, rattled against the hillside and stole any semblance of safety from the tiny cave.

"Is that–?" Medair began, but couldn't finish.

Islantar half-rose, but settled back. "Not human."

"No," Cor-Ibis agreed. "A hunting cry."

"Hunting one of us." Medair had received no replies to her wend-whispers, and was particularly concerned about Ileaha, whose sensitivity to magic might not be enough to lead her to the hill.

"Very likely." Cor-Ibis was sitting closest to the entrance, and she could see his dimly luminescent form leaning forward as he gazed down at the forest. "The mist is lifting."

"They've released whatever it was in those caged caves. The thing which snatches. Or the other." The killer.

"Can we do anything?" Islantar eased alongside Medair so he could look over Cor-Ibis' shoulder.

Cor-Ibis shook his head. "Expose ourselves to the hunter and the guards, though we have little chance of even locating our companions? No." He turned back into the darkness of the cave, getting down to business. "Your reserves are still high, Kierash?"

"Yes. I have done little today but watch the valour of others."

"Then cast wend-whispers, to supplement any lost to the mist. Avahn was with the Mersian Herald and Kaschen las Cormar, so one casting will be sufficient for three. Do you know Ileaha las Goranum well enough for a wend-whisper to find her?"

"I believe so. I have seen her often, though we have not spoken. I cannot say the same of the other two brought to this place."

"Even so, try them both. Tell them where we are and suggest to them, if it is not too late, that they find a high perch in which to shelter for the rest of the night. At the dawn, I will go to the cave behind that spur of rock, to collect any who have reached that far. If they have not reached that point a decem after the break of light, they should make their way without us." He paused, then said: "We cannot leave Estarion unchecked," and if he was unhappy about including the Kierash in any attempt on Castle Gyrfalcon – Falcon Black – he kept his concerns to himself.

"I can keep guard, while you both sleep," Medair said, after the wend-whispers had been cast and Islantar was sampling the eclectic mix of stale food she had offered.

"We will all need our rest," Cor-Ibis said. "Kierash, you are familiar with the detection class?"

"You wish a trip-warning?" Islantar asked, between mouthfuls.

"On the hillside below and above. Then a small shield on this entrance, nothing strong or it will be detected. Enough to give us a few moments, should the hunter stray close."

Despite his youth, Islantar cast with a speed and confidence which far outstripped Medair's abilities. She wondered if he was trying to demonstrate to Cor-Ibis that he was more than capable of defending himself, and that they should concentrate their plans on the major concern: stopping Estarion. That was something Medair could also focus on. However he had achieved it, the Decian King's ability to summon countless gates was a continuing danger to Palladium. And, overriding everything else, was the chance that he would again turn to wild magic, now that his army was gone.

Medair shivered. The shield, a faint murmur which was unlikely to be sensed above the swirl of magic from castle and forest, had blocked the chill wind, but could do nothing to keep away memory. The thick scent of blood rose to stifle her, though the journey through the wet forest must surely have washed her boots clean. But she could not wash away death, thought it would have been like this, no matter who she used the Horn against. Thousands of lives.

The uncomfortable problem of a small cave and a night to pass bothered Medair less now the Kierash was there. Islantar stretched out along one side of the pad of blankets and bedrolls and Cor-Ibis took centre. Medair simply lay with her back to him, glad of her satchel's packrat qualities, which allowed her a blanket to herself. She could not help but think of Avahn and Ileaha and the others, lost in the forest without food or water, let alone blankets. No doubt they would be glad to exchange places with her.

But the scent of blood kept creeping in, and a field of corpses, too many to name. She began to shiver and couldn't stop and when Cor-Ibis reached out she turned and sobbed out her guilt against the chest of a man whose milky radiance would not even allow her to hide from the 'sheer simple fact' of his race. The comfort she found in his arms only made everything worse, but she was glad, when finally there were no tears left, to simply be able to hold him.

He loved her. He had said so. Why should it matter that he was Ibisian, when it did not matter to him that she was Farakkian? There was no enmity between them. But how could she contemplate a relationship with Cor-Ibis when it made her feel so shamed? To lie alive in his arms, with the blood of thousands on her hands?

Avahn had said she could be a unifying force in Palladium, just as the false Medairs had attempted to be the opposite. But that was before she had blown the Horn, an act which would inevitably make her a rallying point for hatred. Wouldn't taking an Ibisian lover do more harm, add insult to impossible injury? Could she stand to be seen that way? She, who had always wanted to follow a right and honourable course? Being anything with Cor-Ibis would give too many an obvious reason for her actions.

Until sleep came to claim her, Grevain Corminevar's words played over and over in her mind:

There was no right choice, messenger. And no wrong decision.

SIX

Morning light scoured the cave of all its secrets. The pad of bedrolls and blankets had flattened wafer-thin, doing little to shield Medair from the uneven floor, and the scratches, bruises and scrapes of the previous night all gave tongue in a minor chorus of pain.

Kierash Islantar lay on his stomach next to her, chin resting on crossed arms as he kept watch, gazing along the base of the hill. He glanced back as she sat up, and she tried not to groan at the creaking and popping of her spine.

"How long ago was dawn?" she asked, excavating sand from her eyes. She felt blasted, battered, but somehow cleaner, better able to deal with what she had done, and might have to face. The air smelled of pine, not blood.

"The time limit is almost up. I have not seen anyone going to the cave."

Medair took refuge in practicality, ferreting through her satchel for breakfast. After quickly finishing her share, she warned him not to turn around, so she could change into fresh clothing. Islantar obligingly kept his eyes fixed on the shadow beneath the spur of rock as he munched on the dry biscuits she had offered.

"When I was nine," he said, after she had stopped moving about, "I decided that Cor-Ibis should be my father." He glanced back, and smiled at her expression. "He is not, of course. He would only have been fourteen when I was conceived. But he is what I wanted my father to be.

"That was the year when Athere heard of nothing but Cor-Ibis, awarded the honours of Keridahl Avec, whose acuity was so profound many believed he could read minds, whose manner was so perfect not the slightest fault could be recorded against him. He is our most powerful adept, perhaps the most capable, certainly one of best respected of the Keridahl.

"That was also the year following the death of his mother and Keris Amaret. Those who did not want to be him spent their time courting him. Potential allies, lovers, those of his family who competed to be named his heir. Even his enemies vied for his attention, each moment of his time, wanting what I wanted: to be special to him, to win him."

Medair received this entirely un-Ibisian speech in silence, and searched for some hint of expression in the youth's profile. "Did you succeed?"

"I have no idea. He is, as I said, perfectly correct, and he has never behaved toward me with anything but the courtesy due the future Kier. He has ever held himself aloof from those who pursue. Immensely frustrating, perhaps even more so for my mother, who disliked my too-apparent quest to capture Cor-Ibis' affection almost as much as his failure to gratify me. It is not how *I* should behave."

Islantar looked over his shoulder at her again, then turned resolutely away. Medair thought of how Cor-Ibis had reacted when he had seen Islantar exposed in the midst of the battle on Ahrenrhen Wall. Concern for the heir, or an instinctive desire to protect a bond he would not acknowledge?

"I ceased pursuit after a while, behaved more appropriately, though I still find myself trying to prove myself to him. If he will not love me as a son, he will as Kier."

"Show," Medair murmured. Islantar turned again, then drew himself up into a sitting position.

"Show?"

"You don't know how he feels, merely what he shows you. And you are talking about this to me because—?"

"Because I cannot be certain you will not attempt to take your life again," Islantar replied, with a note of sorrow. "I think if you ran from him, he would be quite capable of finding you wherever you went. If you were killed, he would bear the wound always, but go on. I do not believe he would survive your suicide. And I do not wish to lose him."

For once, Islantar sounded his age. He looked down, but had recovered his equilibrium by the time Medair could summon a reply.

"I'm not going to kill myself, Kierash," she said, surprised at her own certainty. "I don't know what precisely I will do, but that moment has passed at least." She grimaced. "You remember everything, then? You were very disoriented before."

"For a short time I was the *Niadril* Kier," he said. He lifted a hand, but stopped short of touching his face. "I thought his thoughts, felt what he felt. I do not remember a great deal of his life, only snatches, things which occurred to him while he was...within me. You are very different now, to how he first saw you. He could not decide if you look more or less vulnerable."

Medair winced. "Please. I would prefer it if you didn't tell me things like that."

"The need to demonise the enemy. He understood it." Islantar nodded, then caught himself. "I'm sorry. It was one of the most profound experiences of my life. What could impact me more than being someone else, let alone such a man? I cannot talk about it to anyone else, not in the same way, but I won't keep reviving the past for you."

He turned, looking back towards the spur once again. "There has been some movement down the road from the castle," he told her. "A patrol went past, circling the hill, but did no more than glance cursorily into the caves. The one behind the spur is deep enough to hide a thousand."

Medair, her tentative equilibrium shredded by thoughts of Ieskar, decided that packing would be the most sensible thing to do while they waited. To focus on moving forward, instead of wallowing in the past. She had barely finished when Islantar leaned forward, briefly exposing himself to make some signal.

"He has someone with him, two people," the Kierash said. "We should go down now, carefully."

Following the Kierash out of the cave, Medair craned to see Cor-Ibis' two companions. They were immediately recognisable: the red-haired Velvet Hand, Liak ar Haedrin, and the male kaschen, an Serentel. Her heart was heavy as she eased down among the rocks, keeping behind what little shelter the uneven hillside offered. Avahn and Ileaha had been her companions for weeks, were friends, despite their Ibisian blood. Just as Cor-Ibis, no matter how white his skin, was the man she loved.

Acknowledging that fact didn't diminish the difficulty of her future, but it did allow her to meet his eyes directly, and not flinch away from what had happened between them in the dark. Whatever else, she would not run.

He waited until she was close, then touched the back of her hand. It was the only gesture he allowed himself as they headed into the cave behind the spur, but it was apparently enough for Liak ar Haedrin and an Serentel, who were not nearly correct enough to hide their comprehension. They seemed startled, oddly pleased. Medair again felt that wash of shame, and tried to fight it. They were not enemies, and there was no dishonour in caring for this man.

"We cannot move on until the patrol has passed again," Cor-Ibis said. He was amazingly neat after a night in a cave. Other than some minor stains on his clothing and the livid purple-red scratch from the corner of one eye down to the edge of his jaw, he was as immaculate as ever. Medair was not altogether sure how he had managed it.

The cave entrance curved, so they weren't immediately exposed to outside view, and he stopped as soon as they had travelled far enough for his glow to become noticeable, turning to Medair. "There is not time to fully investigate the various arcana you have brought from Bleak's Hoard, but we should be able to sort out items for immediate use. Kaschen, if you would watch the entrance?"

The young soldier nodded briefly and moved back toward the sunlight. Those left settled themselves on a tumble of flat rocks.

"The most powerful items are best left to another time," Cor-Ibis said. "Such formidable arcana might prove unsafe for us, even if they did not reveal our presence."

Medair wordlessly opened her satchel and brought out a handful of rings. She separated those where she knew the function, and lined them on the rock beside her.

"Animal control, teleport, strength." She poured the rest into his hand. "I don't have the sensitivity for divination, so I was trying to discover their function simply by putting them on."

"Have you tried them all?" he asked, picking out one particularly simple circle of bluish metal and bringing it close to his eyes.

"No, only six. These two gave me no clue to their function. The sixth I tried was the teleport, and after that I decided not to risk any more."

He nodded, handing the bluish ring to Islantar. "You will wear this," he instructed as he put the rest of the rings on the rock beside him, then selected one of silver. Islantar immediately mimicked him, holding the ring close to his face, half-closing his eyes as he concentrated on Cor-Ibis' unspoken test.

"A luck-ring," the boy said, eyes widening. "I thought they were no more than legend."

"But those emanations could be nothing else," Cor-Ibis said. He turned over the silver ring. "This allows the wearer to breathe under water." He handed another ring to Islantar, then started a pile of those they had identified. Medair watched with unconcealed amazement. She had seen adepts puzzle over unidentified arcana for days.

After the luck-ring and the water-breather, there was a poison ward and a thin jewelled band which would summon a mageglow when twisted. Cor-Ibis lingered over two identical rings, then handed one to Islantar and told him to exchange it for the luck-ring, slipping the one he retained onto a finger.

"A wend-whisper?" Islantar asked, after a moment.

"No. Direct communication. So there is a way, after all." Cor-Ibis looked at Medair and smiled, that straightforward expression she still found strange from someone so very Ibisian. "The contents of your satchel make us seem unadept indeed. Luck-rings I had at least heard of, though this is the first hint I've ever discovered of a mage who had succeeded in such a crafting."

"The Hoard was legendary for more than its volume," Medair said.

He nodded, eyes grave, then returned to the rings. There was another invisibility ring and the last, much to Medair's chagrin, was a ward proof against traces.

"If only I'd known that before Vorclase tracked me all the way from Bariback to Finrathlar."

"Hind-sight." Cor-Ibis pocketed the trace-ward, then handed her one of the communicators, not noticing that the word had made her blink.

Kel ar Haedrin was given the strength enhancer, with appropriate warning against its side-effects, and Islantar the invisibility ring to carry. "You must avoid capture above all else," Cor-Ibis said, an unequivocal order.

"I will make that one of my priorities," Islantar replied, equally quiet. They seemed very like father and son at that moment, mirrors of solemn determination and certainty. Then a hurried step from the cave entrance broke the lock of their eyes.

"Keridahl," said Kaschen an Serentel. "One comes. Ibis-lar, but not one I know."

A single commanding gesture saw them all fading into the shadows, behind the rocky outcroppings of the walls. Cor-Ibis' glow was so obvious that, after a moment's hesitation, he walked back out into the centre of the cave. Medair bit her lower lip while the man she didn't want to love stood exposed, unmoving as any statue. The footsteps came closer, paused, moved forward in a determined rush, then paused again.

All eyes were on the bright triangle of sunlight marking the curving cave entrance. First there was a hint of movement, then a shadow which preceded a woman holding a sword at ready. Her braid of pure white hair caught the light as it swung about her ankles. She was as Ibisian as Cor-Ibis, had even a family resemblance, and moved with the grace of the best swordswomen. The clothing she wore was very similar to Liak ar Haedrin's uniform, that of a warrior in Cor-Ibis' private guard. Cool eyes swept the cave, stopping at Cor-Ibis' face.

"'Lukar!" Relieved and pleased, the woman lowered her sword, and hurried forward at a less cautious pace. "I was afraid I had missed you."

"Ileaha." Cor-Ibis said the name slowly. Medair stared.

"Avahn and Heleise and one of the kaschen have been taken," the woman said, her voice admittedly very like Ileaha's. "A patrol of ten from the castle caught them just as they came out of a cave." She shook her head, the ankle-length braid swinging. "They were no more than fifty feet from me the entire night, if only I had known it. Who would have thought a tree would prove the safer?"

"This just happened?" Cor-Ibis asked, ignoring any surprise he might be feeling in favour of more pressing concerns.

"No. Shortly after dawn. I followed them in case there was any chance of breaking them free before they were taken into the castle, but the patrol was alert." The woman took a step forward. "But, 'Lukar, the most important thing: they took them into one of the caves, not the castle. I followed them in and was nearly captured myself when the patrol split, with two remaining with Avahn and the others. Once the rest had resumed circling the castle, I went back into the cave, and found a gate, quite far in. The lock was not one which could be forced, so I came here as quickly as I could."

"The AlKier favours us," Cor-Ibis said. "When the patrol goes past again, we will make our way to this cave, rather than attempt a frontal assault." He gestured to the hidden kaschen, who emerged and returned to the cave entrance to watch, his curiosity and disappointment poorly disguised.

"Ileaha." Medair gave up hiding as well. She searched a stranger's face as she approached. Leaner than the Ileaha she had travelled with to Athere, and the colouring was dramatically different, as perfectly pale as the purest Ibisian. Her thick, silken rope of hair swayed with her every movement. But it *was* Ileaha.

"Medair!" The woman embraced her, much to Medair's discomposure. "I feared we had lost you as well."

"Not quite." Medair glanced at Cor-Ibis, who was watching expressionlessly. "Ileaha, do you remember the Conflagration?"

A frown touched pale blue eyes. "Conflagration?"

"Do you remember the fire surrounding Athere?"

"Estarion's army?" Ileaha was grave, puzzled by the question but answering obediently. "I have never before seen such a display of bale-fire. Tens of thousands of weapons raised against us."

"Do you remember when you met me?"

Ileaha paused, eyes narrowing. "Do you think me an imposter, Medair? Yes, of course I remember when I met you. It was at the Caraway Seed Inn on Thrence Island. Do you have any other questions?"

"Do you recall our departure from Thrence, when we rode north toward Farash?"

The woman who had once been Ileaha stared. "You can't *ride* off an island," she pointed out. "The Alshem took us to the north shore of the Shimmerlan."

Medair touched the warrior woman's arm, more tentatively than she would have the original Ileaha's. "You don't recall the night we stayed in the Whistling Hills? When Avahn recited 'Faron's Lament'? 'The Lady of the Hills'?"

"Avahn is forever repeating some fragment of Telsen," Ileaha said, with a shrug which went awry half-way through. She stared at nothing for a long moment, eyes wide and frightened, raised a hand to her head, and then collapsed. Medair went to her knees as the rest of their small company came out of hiding.

"The transformations of the Conflagration haven't ceased?" Islantar murmured, looking down at the tangle of limbs and braid and Medair attempting to cradle Ileaha's head. "If it has done this, what other unpredictable changes might we face?" Catching Medair's eye, he raised a hand apologetically even as he continued. "And yet, she has not forgotten as completely as N'Taive, who has yet to be brought to recall anything of the person she was before she became the Herald of Tir'arlea."

"Between two worlds." Cor-Ibis helped Medair straighten Ileaha's crumpled form. The woman began to revive as he touched her, but was obviously no longer the warrior who had entered the cave, confident in her past. Her face was slack with horror, and she turned it from Cor-Ibis as if she did not want to look at him.

"Here," Medair said, unsealing her satchel and handing it to him. "Leave me alone with her a while. To locate the objects I described, think of them and reach into the satchel."

"Of course." Cor-Ibis paused, then added gently: "I give you use of my name, Ileaha." He rose smoothly and drew Kel ar Haedrin and Islantar further into the cave.

"Do you want to sit up?" Medair asked. She applied slight pressure to Ileaha's shoulder and started when the woman jerked forward, then struggled quickly to her feet. Taking a few short steps, she clutched at the rough stone wall, eyes pressed tightly shut.

Medair did not immediately disturb her. Then, when it seemed Ileaha would not move, she said, "You remember who you were?"

"I remember who I *am*," Ileaha replied harshly, glaring down at herself. The tip of her braid, clasped by an ornate band of silver, swung mockingly through the shadows. "Who I am, not what has been made of me."

"Is it–?" Medair hesitated. "Maybe you should sit down."

"And that will make it better?" But she did as Medair suggested, staring back into the cave, where Cor-Ibis had summoned a mageglow, since his internal illumination was not enough to offset the gloom.

"Do you remember two lives now?"

"I remember my life. And that of a person who doesn't exist." Ileaha squeezed her eyes shut, then opened them, taking a deep breath. The lines of despair on her face eased as she fought for some measure of self-control.

Medair searched for something useful to say, and tried: "You are probably the only person in all Farakkan who knows and understands the world left by the Conflagration, as well as the one it replaced. That is not...unenviable."

"Hardly."

"Are your two lives so very different?" Medair asked. "You seem to have become what you planned to be, a little sooner perhaps."

Ileaha shook her head. "Don't you see? Medair, if you thought the war which broke the Palladian Empire had been prevented, that the Ibis-lar had accepted the rule of Corminevar, but one day you were among your friends and they said to you something which made you realise that your memories were false, that all you knew were dead, that you were – wrong?"

"An extreme example," Medair said, wishing very much that someone would reveal to her that the past year and five hundred were a figment of her imagination. But – that would mean Cor-Ibis would never have touched her. She backed away from the thought. "Your two lives can't be so unlike as *that*, Ileaha."

"No." Ileaha reached out and clasped Medair's shoulder briefly. "That was thoughtless, Medair. Forgive me."

"There was no offence," Medair said, wondering how close a friendship this new Ileaha remembered them sharing.

"Twenty-three years of being alone, Medair. That is what I have. Of being unworthy, of being one of Cor-Ibis' wards, half-breed in a pure family, unwanted, without value. And this is what I am in the Conflagration's version of Farakkan, where the cold blood does not readily dilute when it mixes with Farakkian heat, and children born of Ibis-lar and Farak-lar show nothing at all of the blood of this land."

She looked down at her hands, long and slim, roughened by the calluses of a sword-fighter. "The worst of it is, I look back at my two pasts and the difference is in how I behaved, not how others did. Oh, I was spared some of it, looking as I now do, but it was my reaction to those around me which altered the whole complexion of my life. One Ileaha believed herself a burden, the other was too busy to care what the smirking maid and the bored governess thought of her. Those two were there in both lives. Everything is remarkably similar, in fact, and the fault was in me. I drew condemnation, practically courted it."

"By lacking confidence? I was a quiet child, Ileaha. I wanted to please my mother, wanted to be the perfect daughter my sister was not. I...like approval, I suppose. I don't like anyone to consider me in the wrong, which makes some–" Medair grimaced. "Trying to be that faultless child just meant I was ignored. So I decided to be the perfect Herald and, though I would be very glad to have found a way to avoid war, to unmake all those deaths, I would not like to do my life over as a bolder, better me, who truly could shine in all her endeavours. That wonderful person I could have been doesn't mean that the person I am is less valuable. You have taken different paths to the same person, and have no reason to despise either course."

"Not the same person, Medair. I am not a Velvet Hand. I have only ever wanted to be on name terms with my guardian, I have never called him 'Lukar to his face. I did not earn the congratulations of the Kier herself, or spend a year in Mylar las Cor-Ibis' bed. I have not–" She broke off, and passed a hand across her face. "All these people, whose memories of their past is different from my own. The worst is Avahn, who I remember as pursuing me relentlessly since he was named heir, and yet has never even thought to do so. The new Ileaha could never take him seriously, and the old? I have loved him since I was a child and never dared to speak, could do nothing but hide behind a pretence of disdain. Now I remember months of courtship. But at least I know the truth, which is better than acting on these false memories."

"Ileaha..."

"No." The hand the young woman held up was as commanding as the Kier's, part of the new Ileaha. "That is enough. I know the truth and I will deal with it. There are far more important matters to think of." She stood, looking at their clustered companions. "What are they doing?"

"Trying to identify some of the invested magic I brought out of Bleak's Hoard," Medair replied, reluctantly. "Before we attempt the castle." Ileaha's skin had an unhealthy waxen sheen and there was something about her which reminded Medair of a dropped vase, reassembled into its former shape but with no glue to hold it together. The cracks showed.

Silently, Ileaha moved to join the others, stationing herself Cor-Ibis' shoulder, firmly relegating herself to somewhere other than the centre of attention. Medair followed helplessly, unable even to comfort the younger woman. Cor-Ibis made no comment, which was probably the best approach. Instead, he handed Ileaha a sheathed sword: long, slim and unadorned.

"This will cut through almost any armor," he told her. "The sheathe seems to be part of the enchantment."

"Thank you, Keridahl," Ileaha replied. No more 'Lukar, it seemed. He asked her about the cave the patrol had used and she plainly found some comfort in reporting matter-of-factly.

"No detectable traps or trips. The gate is in an off-branch of the main cave. There are signs of frequent passage inside, but it is necessary to cross stone to reach the entrance, so there is no trail worn to make that particular cave stand out from its many fellows. It's in the southern face of the hill, more west than east."

"Did you travel at all through the forest on your way here this morning?"

"Only the very periphery. Either the mist is not triggered during the day or I did not venture in far enough."

"Or Estarion has the means to set and unset the enchantment." He handed Medair back her satchel, having provided himself with a sword and Islantar a long knife before replacing the other items. "After such a devastating loss, Estarion's forces cannot be many. The patrol suggests that they are not as disordered as I had hoped, but we are still more likely to encounter servants than soldiers. These can be overpowered, put out of the way. A general alarm should be avoided for as long as possible. Ideally, though it is unlikely, I wish to find and stop Estarion without alerting the castle at all." He paused. "It will be necessary to kill him, not merely rescue our fellows and take whatever means he has to summon gates. It is unlikely Farakkan can survive another wave of wild magic if he is driven to summon it again."

"And after we have killed this man?" Islantar asked. "What then?"

"If we have found a location which can be usefully fortified, Avahn and I will attempt to create a gate boosted by the rahlstones – provided he still has his. Staying together–"

He broke off as an Serentel signalled from the entrance, and they once again took shelter. Booted feet tramped past the cave entrance without pause, and the kaschen signalled again.

"We will go through the forest edge," Cor-Ibis said, leading the way to the entrance of the cave, but not venturing out immediately. "Once in the castle, we must keep together, though it increases our risk of detection. If we cannot finish Estarion, then our goal is

Taedrin City. We will leave the castle as we entered it and, if we are separated, return to this cave for shelter. If it is not possible to regroup, then each is to attempt to make Taedrin City alone, and you especially Kierash. Did you prepare the wend-whisper?"

Islantar nodded.

"Tell Avahn that we are coming for him, and what he should do if he frees himself before we reach him."

Triggering a wend-whisper he had obviously prepared while Medair had been sleeping, Islantar murmured to himself for a short period, then nodded.

"Ready," he said.

Medair hoped they were.

SEVEN

hey scuttled around the base of the hill, keeping to the edge of the trees until Ileaha pointed out a cave, unremarkable among the dozens surrounding it. After scanning the area thoroughly, Cor-Ibis turned his attention to the castle above.

"That turret overlooks this area," he noted. "And, unless I am mistaken, it is currently manned. Cross only on my signal, and quickly."

Medair stared upwards, trying to make out the occupants of the squat tower which projected from the southern wall of the castle. A flash of light reflected from some moving object and Medair found herself utterly certain that she would encounter Estarion's special operative, Captain Vorclase, in Falcon Black. It was he who watched from the turret. She was so confused by this unexpected moment of foresight that she reacted slowly to Cor-Ibis' signal and lagged behind as they crossed. Cor-Ibis questioned her with a touch to her arm, but she shook her head, unwilling to try and communicate such a baseless premonition.

After about forty paces straight in, they needed a mageglow to show the way. Medair then counted another twenty steps before Ileaha indicated a particular side passage. It quickly became obvious that the cave had been widened and smoothed by something other than Farak's decree and by the time they had reached the gate – a series of thick black bars set well into the stone – the walls, ceiling and floor were all even and regular, formed and shaped.

"From here in, stay alert for traps and trips," Cor-Ibis said, running a finger around the keyhole. "Slow progress, but we cannot expect an entrance to the castle to be guarded only by one grid of metal." The lock clicked open and he slowly opened the gate. Medair wondered at the frown which followed, and touched his arm, questioning him in the same fashion he had used. An excuse for a moment's contact, she admitted to herself. He shook his head almost absently, and she guessed that some new concern was troubling him.

The way she and Cor-Ibis were behaving toward each other, as if they had reached some settled accord during her storm of tears, was more than troubling her. She should not allow herself this, not unless she truly believed that she could keep to her resolve.

The enormity of that question was not something she could resolve while trying to invade an enemy castle. The middle of an assassination attempt, and she was focusing on the wrong things. Stopping Estarion, preventing a second wave of wild magic, was the first priority.

"I cannot sense any enchantment in the immediate area," Islantar said, stepping through the gate while Cor-Ibis' attention was on Medair. "But how do we discover snares set without magic?"

"With our eyes," Ileaha said, catching the Kierash's arm before he took another step and indicating the faint outline of a square in the centre of the passage.

"We will need more light, to catch such subtleties," Cor-Ibis said, turning from Medair to make a short sharp gesture. A further two mageglows burst into existence. He looked at his hand strangely, then walked forward. "If you will lead the way, Ileaha, while Kierash Islantar and I concentrate on our senses?"

"Of course, 'Lukar," Ileaha said, prowling forward. Medair saw the young warrior check, as the two pasts in her mind collided again, but then she continued to glide smoothly down the passageway.

They had not moved more than thirty paces past the gate when Cor-Ibis told Ileaha to hold her position.

"A detect," Islantar said, and Cor-Ibis nodded.

"Nothing to impede us," the Keridahl said. "Merely to inform those above of intruders. It will take some little time for me to disable it without alerting Falcon Black."

Without further ado he lost himself in the opening series of gestures for most common spells. After watching him for a short while, Medair belatedly remembered to share around her supplies.

They sat down to eat and wait, all lost in their own thoughts. Islantar was watching her and she wondered if he was not convinced by her assurance that she had no intention of suiciding. That way out now seemed a very pointless thing to do, even if she were no longer a proud Imperial herald, walking confidently down a clear and just path.

"Go through," Cor-Ibis said, the picture of concentration. He waited until they had travelled some distance further before following. Medair's arcane strength was too limited to allow her to sense the detect, but the power must be costing Cor-Ibis to blind it was enough to make her worry about mages in the castle above.

"The tunnel slopes up," Kel ar Haedrin said, but no-one answered. The quiet was unnerving and Cor-Ibis' plan, necessarily vague in the face of so many unknowns, now seemed wholly inadequate. They were outnumbered, even if the patrol and the guards in the blockhouses were all that remained of Estarion's forces. And Vorclase.

Recalling that strange premonition, Medair grew ever more uneasy. Who had said that all the rules had changed? And were still changing. Ileaha had been within the shield wall when the Conflagration had swept over them, but wild magic had found and changed her. Medair didn't want to be reshaped into a different person, even if that person's life was a more pleasant one.

Could she have already been reshaped, less drastically? Where had that certainty come from? She'd never felt so sure of anything in her life as she was of the fact that Vorclase waited in Falcon Black, but she had absolutely no foundation on which to ground her belief. It seemed far more logical for Vorclase to have perished outside Athere with the rest of Estarion's forces.

"Light ahead," Kel ar Haedrin said, after they had ascended almost two full circles, climbing the hill from the inside. Cor-Ibis immediately extinguished two of the mageglows and sent the last darting into one of his sleeves.

"Probably a set light," he said, after they had all had the opportunity to study the faint, steady glow creeping around the curve of the passage. "Kel ar Haedrin, if you would go ahead?"

Kel ar Haedrin nodded and slipped away, keeping as close as possible to the inner wall. There were no cries of alarm, and very quickly she was back.

"Another gate, Keridahl. A stair is beyond, and other gates. But no guard. I did not go close enough to sense if there is a trip."

"Very well. Stay here."

He took the remaining mageglow with him, leaving them in darkness. Medair took the jewelled ring from her satchel and summoned another glow.

"Another trip," Cor-Ibis said, voice floating back to them. He was quicker this time, and soon they stood clustered around the base of a stair streaked with moisture. Water dripped from cracks and crevices in the ceiling and there were several other gates, all firmly locked.

Beside two of them were bins which contained a collection of grains and root vegetables. Picking out a withered parsnip, Ileaha moved towards one of the gates, then stopped.

"This seems to lead to the predator which hunted last night," she said, eyeing dark stains on the ground. "The blood traces are old."

"Not recently fed," murmured Kel ar Haedrin, as Ileaha moved to the next gate and peered into the darkness beyond.

"Nothing moving," Ileaha said, tossing the parsnip through the bars so that it lay just within the strips of light cast by their mageglows. She tugged at the bars, and found them firmly seated. "If these were unlocked, escape this way will be difficult."

Cor-Ibis examined the lock to the predator cave, then said a word beneath his breath and watched it melt into uselessness. He repeated the process with the next lock but left the gates which did not obviously lead to an animal lair. Then he sent Kel ar Haedrin and Ileaha on their way up the stairs. Islantar was corralled in the centre of the group, as protected as possible.

The stair doubled back on itself repeatedly, the narrow steps worn and slippery. Medair was last in line, keeping nervously close to the kaschen immediately in front of her. She did not like the darkness nipping at her heels, and directed the mageglow she had summoned to trail rather than lead her.

Just as she reached the first landing, a whining growl, high and vicious, rose out of the dark. Kaschen las Cormar immediately drew his sword and moved to Medair's side.

"It isn't the hunting cry," Medair said, not sounding nearly as confident as she would like. "It must be able to smell us, but not get out of its cage."

The kaschen looked up the stair to Cor-Ibis, who nodded once and gestured for them to move on. Medair decided she should take this as a sign that he trusted her judgment. That mattered to her. She wished she could keep her thoughts from the silent question he posed. Far, far too many things had happened in the last day, and until she had a chance to sit down and decide how to feel about it all her heart would continue to trip and stumble and demand she give it thought. And yet the long wait at each obstacle gave her imagination too much opportunity to play with less pleasant futures than one which featured Illukar las Cor-Ibis.

Without doubt all Decia would want her dead, and here she was at its heart, giving them further reason to hate. Off to kill a king because the possible consequences of not doing so were unthinkable. Always, instead of the best, she found herself struggling to make the least-worst decision.

They travelled four flights of slippery steps, then stopped. Medair was too far back to see the problem, and guessed that the extended delay meant they'd encountered another door or trap. Faintly, she could sense magic at work and took a step back to give those above her room to move.

The wait was a long one, and involved several whispered discussions. Finally, there was a too-loud click, then the stair was bathed in the light of day rather than mageglows. Swift movement, and a jingling thud, told Medair the door had been guarded, and that guard had been dispatched.

Then they were moving up and out into a brightly-lit corridor. Squinting as her eyes adjusted to sunlight, Medair looked back at the heavily-bound door through which she had just passed, then to either side. Ileaha was a short distance to her right, standing over the body of a guard.

"Find a place to put him," Cor-Ibis ordered, surveying the corridor. The guard had been running toward a junction further to the right. To the left was a flight of stairs, and a window.

"Medair, do you have anything I can bind him with?" Ileaha asked, dragging the man toward the cave stair.

Faintly relieved to discover Ileaha hadn't simply killed him, Medair helped tie the guard's hands and feet and gagged him with an old kerchief. "You won't be able to do that with everyone we meet," she commented, as they closed the door on the figure lying uncomfortably on the damp stair.

Ileaha nodded. "I've always preferred not to kill by stealth, if the level of risk allows other options," she said, signalling Kel ar Haedrin with three precise hand gestures. It was obviously a command. With an ambiguous shift of expression Kel ar Haedrin obeyed, moving silently to the corner of the junction and peering around it with the aid of a tiny mirror.

"There will be barracks and cells on this level, 'Lukar," Ileaha went on, clipped and assured. "But Estarion might choose to keep a prize like Avahn closer, in the interrogation chambers mentioned in your report on Falcon Black. I would recommend the stair rather than venturing among the barracks."

"Estarion is the one we must reach first," Cor-Ibis said, accepting without comment the role Ileaha now played. "With our companions so recently captured, there is every chance we will find him with them."

Ileaha's assurance had dropped away, two pasts warring behind her eyes, but she nodded and firmed her jaw beneath Cor-Ibis' steady gaze. "The interrogation room is two levels above us. You – your report spoke of the area being heavily guarded, but outside the most frequented areas of the castle."

"Then lead us, and quickly. If we can achieve our object before being discovered, we have more chance of winning free alive."

"Keridahl." Kel ar Haedrin had rejoined them, frowning. "There is something you should see."

Both Cor-Ibis and Ileaha followed Kel ar Haedrin back to the corner, used the mirror to spy without being seen, then returned.

"They are working on the equipment of one of the metal giants we faced on the wall," Cor-Ibis said. "Bolting the mail together. It is almost complete."

"They are called *skensai*," Ileaha said, with equal calm. She had apparently come to some internal resolution about her role, enough to explain what Cor-Ibis should know in this remade world. "It takes a life sacrifice to animate one, but the casting is within the power of even a minor adept willing to risk an exacting spell. Our best estimate of Estarion's abilities gives him the power to create at least three *skensai* in a single day, provided he has at his disposal both suitable vessels and the souls to fuel them."

"Life sacrifice?" Islantar murmured. "This I cannot like. Not when our companions are in Estarion's power."

"No." Cor-Ibis imbued the word with a world of meaning. They didn't linger, mounting the stair as soon as it had been cleared of any suspicion of enchantment and climbing the two flights without hindrance.

The stairs opened onto a long, empty corridor which continued around a corner to their right. There was a single door opposite. Ileaha immediately crossed to it and pressed her ear to the fine-grained wood. She signalled that it was clear and, when Cor-Ibis made no objection, opened the door.

"Perhaps not an ideal haven," Ileaha said, surveying the long, panelled room dominated by a highly polished table. There were windows to the left, another door opposite and an archway to their right. Neither secluded nor defensible.

"Keep moving," Cor-Ibis told them, indicating the opposite door, rather than the archway. They hurried across, keeping an eye on the arch as they circled the table. Distantly, Medair could hear a man and woman's voices, rising and falling in conversation. It sounded as if the speakers were at the bottom of the stair she could see through the arch. It only needed a single person to see them and call for help, to make their task infinitely more difficult.

They came out into another corridor, this time with two young women half-heartedly mopping the floor, their faces streaked with tears. Ileaha and Kel ar Haedrin moved in blurred unison, each taking a struggling armful before either maid had a chance to so much as squeak. Only a mop, clattering to the ground, spoiled the silence of the manoeuvre.

"More rope," Ileaha said imperatively, controlling the struggles of her captive with ease.

While the maids were bound and gagged, Islantar investigated the nearest doors and finally opened the end-most onto an empty bedroom. They stowed the maids and continued quickly down the corridor. At this rate, Medair reflected, they would be discovered by the trail of trussed castle inhabitants left in their wake.

"This must be it," Kel ar Haedrin murmured, using her mirror to look beyond the corner at the end of the corridor. "Doors barred from the outside, and one of them guarded. The guard is some thirty, forty paces from us. The corridor widens to the left further on – I cannot see what lies there."

"The invisibility ring," Medair suggested. Cor-Ibis nodded.

"We are painfully exposed here," Islantar whispered, glancing back toward the dining room after handing Ileaha the ring.

"If we are discovered, we can push further in and attempt to barricade," Ileaha replied, almost too softly for Medair to hear. "Retreat down those stairs will gain us little, and being hunted through those woods, having the countryside raised against us, would be close to suicide."

She put on the ring and faded, while they waited, watching forward and back, without even a hint of a footstep to mark her departure, or progress.

The pause stretched, and they balanced on a knife-edge. Any Decian entering the corridor behind them would see them while still out of immediate reach, and the guard around the corner was too far to risk trying to rush. They could cast Sleep at him instead, but it was not a quiet magic, and still Ileaha did not make her move. All they could do was listen to the man shift wearily, scratching at some itch. They could not even look at him for fear of being seen in return; only Kel ar Haedrin was able to watch.

A distant noise, like paper falling to the floor, came, but Kel ar Haedrin shook her head. Medair silently counted to ten to keep herself still, and on nine heard the unmistakable sound of a body falling to the ground, and Ileaha's voice, saying softly: "Clear."

When Medair rounded the corner, Ileaha was carefully cleaning a small knife, and the figure at her feet was as still as Jedda las Theomain had been. And Jedda was another thing Medair needed to consider, when circumstances gave her time to focus her thoughts. She should not forget that she was not necessarily safe among Ibisians.

A glance down the corridor showed an open area, a station for the guards who watched over the interrogation rooms. One booted foot was all that was visible to suggest another crumpled figure. The work of a Velvet Sword.

Kel ar Haedrin was already working on the bar of the door. In a matter of moments they had it open. The room beyond was small, and lushly overwhelmed by a cushioned bed, rugs, a soft chair. It was a prison with all the accoutrements of the bedchamber of a noblewoman, including the noblewoman.

EIGHT

The woman was perhaps forty. She stood very upright in the centre of the room, arms folded. The room was obviously a cell, despite its luxuries, but the woman's stance was as imperious as an Empress in her throne room.

After a pause, Cor-Ibis said: "Princess Sendel?"

"As you see, Keridahl," the woman replied, coldly. She surveyed their small band, eyes disdainful in a thoroughly Decian face: bronze skin, high cheekbones and a hawk nose. Her composure was formidable, though it cracked when she discovered Islantar at Ileaha's elbow. She eyed the boy in surprise, then turned back to Cor-Ibis. "This is not a counter strike."

"Not precisely, Highness," Cor-Ibis replied, ever-courteous. "Your brother's forces were defeated, and he struck at us with a gate as he fled, transporting us here. We have eluded capture, thus far."

"Have you indeed?" The princess strode out of the cell and looked around impatiently, unperturbed by the corpse which lay on the floor. "A quick and decisive battle, it must have been. Well, you need not fear that I will raise the alarm. I objected to Xarus' latest scheme, and rightly so, it sounds to me. He saw fit to confine me here. Expanding Decia's borders is one thing; throwing everything into a fool's obsession with the past is another. How many Decian born did he waste against Athere's walls?"

"There were very few survivors," Cor-Ibis replied.

"And he has slunk back to lick his wounds? Your abduction would be, what, an attempt at revenge or a clutch for bargaining chips?" The princess did not hide her disgust. "Defeat is not a thing Xarus has ever been able to accept. He will not treat you kindly if you are captured."

"No." Cor-Ibis glanced at Ileaha, indicating that she should check the other rooms. "Three of our party have been captured, and we must continue to seek them out. Please accept our protection, if you wish it."

Princess Sendel looked amused. "You may accept mine, Keridahl. There are those still loyal to me in Falcon Black, and I have no interest in prolonging hostilities with Palladium."

As Cor-Ibis negotiated polite obligation with the princess, Kel ar Haedrin opened another of the rooms off the corridor, revealing a Decian youth of about sixteen. His fine tailoring was crumpled, and he eyed the small band of Ibisians with disbelief. One hand strayed to his side, instinctively seeking an absent sword, but Princess Sendel forestalled any confrontation, turning from Cor-Ibis to eye the young man disdainfully.

"You, here?" she asked. "What became of your ambition to stride through the ashes of Athere?"

The youth glanced at Ileaha's bared sword, held far too close for any enemy's comfort. A shift of his coppery features revealed a distinct resemblance to Princess Sendel. Her son, Medair guessed.

"It remains," he said, with grim resolve. "I will see the rightful heir on the Silver Throne."

"Yet you are here," the princess repeated.

"My heart might be with my uncle's cause, Madam, but my duty lies with you," said the youth. "I could not fight at his side while he had you imprisoned."

"Vastly pretty," said Princess Sendel, contemptuously. "Fortune favours you, Thessan. This affecting sentiment appears to have saved your life."

"There is no-one else here, Keridahl," Kel ar Haedrin said in an undertone, as Thessan stared at the princess.

"What do you mean?" he demanded. "Where is the King?"

"Would that I knew." Princess Sendel gathered up her skirts, out of the path of the thin line of blood advancing from the guard's body. "We will find him, shall we? And ask of his war, of his splendid victories?"

"Princess, we must search for our companions," Cor-Ibis said, ignoring the exchange. "Can you suggest where they might be held?"

"The cliff cells, most likely," Princess Sendel said, earning a scandalised look from her son.

"Mother, you can't aid the enemy!" he said, shifting uneasily between Ileaha and Kel ar Haedrin. His gaze settled on Cor-Ibis. "Why are you here, White Snake?" he spat. "Have you run from Decia's soldiers to try and strike at Falcon Black?"

"At this moment, I seek only three of my own," Cor-Ibis said, mildly. "Ileaha, if you would be so good?"

Obediently, Ileaha gripped Thessan's arm and propelled him firmly back toward the cell.

"Wait!" he protested. "At least tell me how the battle progresses! Have Athere's walls been breached yet?"

"No." Medair spoke quietly. "The war is over, the battle lost. Athere stands. I sounded the Horn of Farak and Decia no longer has an army."

Thessan flinched, incredulity warring with fury as he stared at her. Then he surged forward and spat. Moisture flecked Medair's cheek even as Ileaha quickly pulled him back, then closed and locked the door.

"Medair– " Ileaha began, but Medair shook her head.

"That is something I cannot hide from," she said, wiping her face with tired deliberation. She could feel Cor-Ibis at her back, not touching her, but close by. "My choice cost their lives."

"Medair an Rynstar." Princess Sendel eyed Medair with lively interest, but not the hatred displayed by her son. "None of the tales of your rebirth suggested you would side with the Ibisians."

"With Palladium," Medair corrected. She was slowly finding it easier to accept that decision, or futile to continue to argue against herself, since it was beyond her power to change. Her Emperor had not given her absolution, had not provided the certainty of right and wrong, but hind-sight was offering her no better choice, much as she would be hated for it. She turned slightly, so that she could see Cor-Ibis' expressionless face. "I could not watch Athere fall."

"You should find Xarus' protégé, the one he thinks belongs on Palladium's throne," the princess said. Dark Decian eyes studied Medair. "But perhaps that issue is dead, now."

80

"Perhaps," Medair said. Killing the supposed descendant of her Emperor, rightful heir or not, was another thing she could not think too hard on, until it was time to face it.

There was little of subterfuge in Princess Sendel's progress. She marched off down the corridor and collared the first person she encountered, a man whose arms were full of silver candlesticks. He seemed more afraid of Sendel than the Ibisians cautiously following the princess.

"Where is my brother?" the princess asked, as the man dropped most of the candlesticks on the floor. He gulped, looked left and right, then said weakly: "The King is dead."

Princess Sendel received the news with no sign of grief or pleasure. "Are you certain?" she asked, stepping forward to further overwhelm the man.

"Yes, Highness." The man licked his lips, eyes darting to Ileaha's bared sword. "Commander Vorclase received a wend-whisper, not a decem ago. The message said that everyone was dead, that the King was dead, the entire army. Everyone."

"Vorclase?"

"H-he said we were to carry out the King's standing orders," the man said, eyes dropping to the pile of candlesticks in a manner which suggested they had nothing to do with anyone's orders. Sendel didn't seem to notice.

"The Four spare me from loyal men," she said, and turned to Cor-Ibis. "This changes matters, somewhat."

"Yes. Your Majesty."

Islantar spoke before Cor-Ibis could say more.

"If King Xarus died on the battlefield," the Kierash said. "Who summoned the gate which brought us here?"

⚬⚭⚬

Estarion had no issue, which meant Sendel was now Queen. She made short work of taking control, simply commandeering everyone they encountered. No-one resisted, despite her Ibisian escort. Vorclase had apparently vanished after passing on the news, failing to leave anyone in command. Sendel rolled over the few remaining castle inhabitants as inexorably as the Conflagration.

Abruptly, in the middle of ordering a search for Vorclase, Sendel stopped and turned to Cor-Ibis. "We had best see about these friends of yours," she said. "It occurs to me that Xarus' standing orders for the treatment of captives may not be benefiting them."

By this time, she had collected quite an entourage, but still led them personally, back down the stairs, passing the door they had used to enter Falcon Black. The guard Ileaha had overcome was probably still behind it. They entered the barracks without opposition, ignored the half-constructed shell of the silver giant and strode through empty rooms.

The cliff cells were precisely that: tiny chambers chipped into stone, high up one side of the rock the castle stood upon. They were rough and cramped, and a cold wind gusted through the crude barred windows. There was not even room for pallets, and their occupants were sitting with their knees up against their chins and their hands in blockish manacles. Only the Mersian Herald and the other kaschen. Avahn was not there.

"Keridahl." Herald N'Taive looked worn and hungry, but otherwise unaffected by her capture. She quickly took in the sight of Ileaha and Kel ar Haedrin still armed amidst the Decian escort, then bowed her head politely to Sendel. "They took Kerin Avahn through there," she said, indicating a solid door at the end of the row of cells.

The new Queen looked at Cor-Ibis. "Kerin Avahn? You seem over-burdened by heirs on this venture, Keridahl." She gestured to one of her followers to free the Herald and the kaschen, and another to open the end door. "My brother called this the steeping room," the Queen continued, and her eyes were grim. "I will give you this comfort, Keridahl. Xarus required them alive for the next stage of this process."

After such encouraging words, Medair could only stare toward the room in horror. Cor-Ibis and Ileaha had both moved quickly forward and disappeared beyond, and Medair followed as if on leading-strings.

It smelled of herbs, and a fresh, strong breeze gusted in through the windows. The room was full of benches and sinks, vats and glassware. Avahn was in the centre, shut within a box formed entirely of glass. He was naked, unconscious, and almost completely submerged in a virulent blue gel. Only his face unsubmerged, his head supported by a small block beneath his neck.

"Open it." Ileaha's voice cracked with horror. Not waiting for help, she tried to wrench the lid off the box and it shifted slightly, obviously heavy. A wave of odour escaped into the room. More herbs, with an acrid underlay which burnt the nose. Cor-Ibis came to Ileaha's aid and together they lifted the lid away, and lowered it to one side. The scent immediately thickened and Medair's eyes filled with tears, as if she were cutting onions. She tried to breathe shallowly, imagining what it must be like for Avahn, completely immersed in the noxious stuff.

"Find my brother's assistants," the Queen ordered, sending a few of her entourage scuttling. "And fetch water." Her nose wrinkled in distaste. "Xarus kept a few close to help him with his experiments. They may know how to undo this."

"This is not an enchantment," Cor-Ibis said, touching Avahn's forehead carefully. "Some kind of drug?"

Ileaha, her face pinched, simply hauled Avahn out of the box and deposited him on one of the benches. She began to cough, her eyes streaming, and turned away to gasp for air. "Some kind of poison." She was liberally smeared with the blue gel.

Against the background of Sendel's no-nonsense commands, Ileaha, Medair and Cor-Ibis rubbed Avahn clean and sluiced him off. He did not so much as stir. He *was* breathing, if shallowly, but his temperature was high and he quickly began to stream with sweat. Even from her brief unshielded exposure Ileaha found that she could no longer feel her hands and felt nauseated, but she did not seem to sicken further. Estarion's assistants could not be found.

"They will be located," Queen Sendel said, standing in the doorway as Kel ar Haedrin and one of the kaschen replaced the glass lid in the hopes of cutting down the fumes. "Vorclase, too, will be fetched back. Our doctors may be able to do something, if any escaped conscription. Until then–" She shook her head. "I have much to do. Accept my hospitality, Keridahl, and when there is less confusion, we will treat for Decia's future."

Cor-Ibis hesitated, and Medair guessed that he was not happy to have Islantar guesting in Decian territory, even at such a juncture.

"You doubt?" Sendel asked, not surprised. "We have no army. Our allies gave as many men as they could spare. To threaten you, let alone your collection of heirs, would only invite retribution, and no kidnap plot could rescue us from that. At this point Keridahl, to save Decia from Palladian retaliation, I would happily accept truth spell or even geas. You will not take harm from me, and I will take every measure I can to ensure that my word is kept by those I command."

There was a short pause, then Cor-Ibis nodded. "We will come to some arrangement," he said.

Sendel did not seem offended. "Wise of you."

"We must discover who brought us here," Cor-Ibis continued. "The question of what created those gates is of highest importance. I am uneasy."

"More searching," Sendel said, not visibly impressed. "We will turn out the caves beneath the castle, if it seems necessary. But first, let us break bread, and gather our strength."

NINE

The spasms always started with a trembling in the hands, which gave them just enough warning to reach the bed before Avahn's back snapped into an arch. His feet drummed against the bed-board, the veins stood out in his throat, and his face turned an alarming purple shade. Then, just when it seemed as if he would vibrate off the bed despite their best efforts, he would go limp and they would anxiously check to see if he was still breathing. It had gone on all day.

"They're getting weaker," Medair said this time, as Avahn turned from iron to jelly beneath her hands. Ileaha didn't answer. Exhausted, her eyes swollen pink from exhaustion and the effects of the poisons Avahn's body was trying to purge, she was focused on her task to the exclusion of all else. Filling the basin again, she silently handed Medair a cloth and together they bathed him, washing away the oily sweat. Then they soaped and cleaned their hands, over and over, until they no longer felt quite so numb and the acrid odour was almost gone.

They'd had no help from a Royal Physician, who had been rousted from some hidey-hole to do little more than tell them all the things he didn't know and make contradictory guesses. Amid suggestions to keep Avahn warm and keep him cool, and cup him and dose him with purgatives, all they could do was keep him clean and pray.

Were weaker seizures a good or bad sign? Medair tried to decide, anxiously watching Ileaha watching Avahn. It was easier to see her *as* Ileaha now that the change in colouring was not so new. She had almost the same face, even if the height was all wrong, and that hair. Her attention never drifted for an instant, as if she were intent on capturing every moment of Avahn's ordeal. Every moment of–

That train of thought was interrupted by the door opening, and Cor-Ibis, followed by Kel ar Haedrin, entered. He crossed to Avahn who, after only a few decems, seemed to have already lost weight. Cor-Ibis' face became particularly blank as he studied his heir, whose colour was a sickly greenish-white shade that made him look like he was decaying inside his own skin.

"Kel ar Haedrin will watch over Avahn now."

Despite Ileaha's obvious reluctance, he led them to a room where the rest of the Palladians waited to sit down to a meal delivered by Decian servants who made little effort to conceal stony animosity.

"Hold," he said when they were alone, and quietly cast. Poison detect, which made every sort of sense. Queen Sendel might have declared them guests, but no Queen had the power to order her people to forgive and forget a field of blood. He followed it with a second casting, one which brought a hush which reminded Medair of the muffling effect of the mist. Something to prevent eavesdropping.

"Queen Sendel has accepted a geas," he said, nodding to give them permission to eat. "That in no way binds the rest of Decia, so we will continue to take as many precautions as is feasible. I have recovered the rahlstone which was in Avahn's custody, and tomorrow morning when we are both rested, the Kierash and I will attempt to construct a gate to Athere. All will return but Kel ar Haedrin and myself." He added a glance at Islantar which was an order, absolute no matter what their ranks. "I cannot move from Falcon Black until we are certain that the device used to create the gates – for Queen Sendel has confirmed the existence of a device – is not here, and that any information King Xarus may have collected regarding the summoning of wild magic is destroyed."

"A wend-whisper from my – the Kier – reached me during the afternoon," the Kierash put in. "Sent shortly after our disappearance. Others may arrive with further information, particularly if the gate-caster was discovered outside Athere's walls."

"We will use the rooms alongside Avahn's," Cor-Ibis continued. "The entrance to that corridor can be effectively guarded, and the kaschens and Kel ar Haedrin will mark shifts overnight."

"I can help with that," the Mersian Herald offered. "My skill with the sword is only moderate, but I will at least serve as a second pair of eyes."

Medair ate with a sense of unreality, listening to Cor-Ibis answering a handful of questions from Islantar regarding the search of the castle. She could not argue with the basic sense of his plan, but wanted to. To leave him here! But he was right, absolutely right, that the gate device needed to be found. Not only so it could not again be used against Athere, but because the question of how it had been created needed to be settled. And Medair had to go, for though they had taken some small precautions against making clear her identity to the majority of Falcon Black's occupants, she knew it would be as great an act of stupidity for her to stay as it would be for Islantar.

When the meal was over, Ileaha joined Kel ar Haedrin caring for Avahn. The doors of all the rooms along the corridor were standing open and, aware that Cor-Ibis was dividing his attention between her and Islantar, Medair walked randomly through one and closed it behind her, to sit blankly and try to force herself to think.

Her role had run its course. She no longer had the Horn. She no longer had the secret of her past, and no-one would think of rallying around her name. Herald no longer. But she did not want to die. So it became a matter of choosing how to live.

Outside, doors closed. After a long pause she could hear Cor-Ibis talking to the Mersian Herald and the first of the kaschen who was to guard the corridor leading to their rooms. A long night for them on top of a tense day, but there was no-one else to trust. Medair listened to one last door close, and then she stood by her window remembering a soft voice say: "Please, Medair."

He had made his position very clear. And she could hardly deny that she wanted to be with him. She was past any self-delusion on that front. But wanting him and making a life with him did not follow in easy progression and she was not cruel enough to go to him now unless she had conquered these interminable doubts. He didn't deserve to have her taking temporary solace from him.

And she was undoubtedly the coward Ieskar had named her, because what held her back now was not any belief that she was still bound by vows to the past, but what others would think of her. Awful as using the Horn had been, she still did not see how she could have done anything except support Palladium over Decia. But though she did not believe that decision was pinned to her feelings for one particular Palladian, there would be all too many who would never accept any other explanation.

Her old pride hated the idea   Medair an Rynstar turning her back on the true Corminevar bloodline because she wanted to spread her legs for a White Snake. Seduced by the enemy. She was already so detested, so loathed, and doubted she was equal to standing before people like Thessan Estarion as they embroidered their hatred for her with such an ugly embellishment. There was no way to make them see that what she felt for Cor-Ibis truly was separate from her decision about the Horn of Farak.

And some part of her must believe it to be true, for she was still so frantically trying to draw back from him that she continued to think of him as 'Cor-Ibis'. He was Illukar. He had held out his hand and she longed to take it and did not. What reason was there? Only this need to wallow in guilt, and cling to an image of honour unsullied by failure. Not wanting to die, but not able to move beyond the past. Caring what people like Thessan Estarion would think was pointless and craven and she could not help it. Proud little Herald, putting on a show for the crowd. Former Herald, false hero, counterfeit legend.

Nor could Medair deny that, quite aside from anyone else's opinion, it still mattered to her that he was Ibisian. He was a White Snake.

Deep down, she knew his greatest fault was that he was too like Ieskar for her to ever be quite comfortable wanting him. "You do not like to face certain truths," Ieskar had said, standing dead in the Hall of Mourning. He'd made her take his hand, and told her she had no reason to hate the people of this time, and it was a thing she knew in her head was true and in her heart was at least mostly true. The war was long over and Ibisians weren't the enemy any more. She closed her eyes and pictured her hand against Ieskar's, and his eternally calm voice telling her that what she felt was hate.

It was a line of thought she simply could not pursue, and she consoled herself with the fact that Ieskar had never smiled as Illukar did. And she was still standing here by the window.

Had she let desire influence her decisions? Would she have given the Horn of Farak to Ibisians if Illukar las Cor-Ibis had been something other than everything she admired? Because if it was true, then she already had cause to be ashamed and it did not matter if no other person ever knew that she loved a White Snake, for she knew herself. And if her decision to give up the Horn was not tainted, because the Palladian Ibisians were not accountable for the past, then how could loving a Palladian Ibisian be any less free from taint?

And could she go round the circle of doubt yet again? What was a little extra scorn to add to the loathing she had already earned? The Medarists, the Hand, the Decians. Did she imagine that anything she did could actually make them hate her more? The only question was what she wanted to be, for what remained of her life. Did she want to be so small as to turn away from what Illukar las Cor-Ibis offered her, just because half the world might disapprove? Just because it was easier not to try and stop hating herself?

This was enough to get her into the hall, walking quietly so as not to give the two on guard reason to turn. But she paused at his door, trying to face the enormity of this decision. This wasn't just for the night. Did she want to be known as Cor-Ibis' leman? Or was it to be a marriage, full formality, everything? Did she actually contemplate having his children?

The memory of Cor-Ibis' marriage, and the fact that it was widely believed he could not father a viable child, quite disrupted her ambiguous feelings. There was considerably more disappointment than relief tangled in that morass, and she thought that maybe it was simpler to accept that she wanted to spend her life with him and save the details for less uncertain times.

The door handle turned silently and she moved forward to see him standing candle-lit at his window. He was combing his hair: a mundane, everyday act made magical as much by his innate poise as the glow which had lit him since he shielded Athere. Medair stood motionless, watching the elegant tilt of his head, those long fingers holding the comb, and his cool, delicate profile. The painful scratch across his cheek was no longer so livid and did not stop him from being utterly beautiful.

The latch clicked as she closed the door and he turned and looked at her, his expression not changing one iota. But he held himself so very still. Naturally, she couldn't begin to think of what to say next and deflected the subject of the future with questions about now.

"Have they found any sign of Vorclase?"

"No." Cor-Ibis put the comb down on a desk, expressionless. Her own face felt stiff and unhappy and she knew she could still walk out, but if she did she should never come back.

"Falcon Hill is a warren," he went on, smoothly enough. "And Estarion has traps and trips laced throughout. It may take days to find him."

"Do you trust Queen Sendel?" Her voice quavered, making her feel stupidly young. She wanted to touch him and was suddenly, unreasonably, afraid of rebuff.

"I took care in forming the geas." Cor-Ibis raised an equivocal hand. "Her previous incarnation was less forthright, but equally pragmatic. Herald N'Taive tells me this version has long been at odds with her brother, yet unwilling to act directly against him. I trust Sendel's grasp of the situation, at least. Turning on us would only make matters worse for Decia. But there are others here who will see less clearly. The Kierash is a natural target." He moved to one side, offering her the chair from the desk. It was easier to sit than to continue to shift from foot to foot, trying to hide her nervousness. Cor-Ibis sat on the bed. "And you are in danger, of course," he said. "If word of your identity spreads."

"I know. And Avahn–" she began, and stopped, for it was no better a topic. She could not quite contemplate talking about Avahn's possible demise. Like too many people, she had not had a chance to say goodbye to him.

"I examined him before I came here," Cor-Ibis told her, his attention never wavering from her face. "What little I could do, I have done. He seems to be breathing easier."

Medair nodded, then looked down at his hands, resting lightly on his knees. There was an awkward pause.

"Gates are beyond the Kierash's casting rank," he said, again filling the breach. "But he is exceptional, and I believe there is a good chance we will succeed tomorrow morning. If not, I have sent a wend-whisper to the Kier, suggesting a gate be opened from Athere."

It was stupid to sit here making conversation. She cast about for some way to ease into talking about overcoming the past. And found herself asking, with appalling bluntness, "Why did your wife hate you?"

Shocked at her own words, she jerked her eyes up to meet his, and saw sudden distance. He took a moment before he replied.

"It is something you need to know," he said, and there was only the barest hint of reluctance in his voice. He shook his head when she started to stammer a denial. "Amaret. My mother recommended her to me. A *sha-leon* marriage, a business contract. They are still common. Amaret was an accomplished adept and, most important to my family, her blood was pure." He glanced at Medair. "My mother chose my father on the same basis. There are arguments that it keeps the blood more powerful, but it is essentially founded on a belief in Ibisian superiority, and entrenched tradition. At twenty–" He shrugged minutely. "I had never thought of love and saw no reason not to marry this particular woman."

"Did she feel the same way?" Medair asked. Her throat was tight. This was not how she had wanted to do this.

"Before the marriage, she gave no sign of wishing anything else. She was little interested in me, and apparently willing to treat the arrangement like the contract it was. In some *sha-leon* marriages, the couple comes together only for the making of children and I cannot say we did more than that. It was an alliance of convenience.

"Early on, I suspected she was unhappy, but it was not until she lost the second child that I realised it was more than dissatisfaction." He met her eyes again, his own frank. "I will not pretend I was not at fault. I was caught up in my studies, cared for little else, and was quite simply not interested in her. I was polite to her when I should at least have tried to make her my friend. After the second child's loss, I tried to reach out, but she made it clear she considered it an intrusion. I thought she was mourning the miscarriages, as only natural, and I let her be." He paused, and she saw a muscle jump in his cheek. That mild voice was even softer than usual. "I did not know how truly she hated me until after my mother's death."

"When she told you she was carrying someone else's child." How must he have felt?

Cor-Ibis shook his head. His gaze was on his hands, lashes shading grey eyes which were strangely blank. "I knew of her affairs, suspected that the third child was not mine. No. That was when she told me she had not miscarried. That she had aborted them."

Medair could only stare at his lowered head. Then, when she could bring herself to speak at all, the only thing she could say was: "*Why?*"

"Because they were mine." The delicate mouth twisted and he looked abruptly tired, like someone who had risen with the dawn in enemy territory and not had a moment to stop since. "She had a secret, Amaret. Her family had some tiny strain of Farak-lar blood, and to them the keeping of that secret was the most important thing in existence. 'They bleached their brows', as a courtier would say. Then my mother approached them with a *sha-leon* proposal, with the Cor-Ibis fortune and title at her back.

"Amaret loathed me because she lived in eternal fear of being discovered by me. The babes were part of me, and would almost certainly reveal her. She told me that she had killed her own children as if it were the proudest thing she had ever done, and wept while she told me because killing them had wounded her so deeply she no longer cared who knew her blood."

He stopped, breathing deeply. Swallowed. His head was bowed to shield a naked hurt kept to himself for too many years. When he spoke again, his voice was uneven. "If she had only asked me, I could have told her how little her blood mattered to me. That it was a tradition I have never embraced. But she did not, and I looked to her only often enough to fulfil my role, not to see how frightened she was. It is the greatest wrong I have ever committed.

"After that, I could not contemplate another contract. There were heirs in other branches of the family, though if I had anticipated the pressures which would be brought to bear on some of my younger cousins, I might have arranged matters differently."

His voice trailed away and he sat watching his hands. She could feel his anguish and lashed herself for making him relive such a horrible discovery. She did not know whether to hate Amaret or pity her.

"Illukar," she said, barely managing to get the whole word out. He looked up quickly, the movement wholly disjointed. He had laid himself bare, scoured his reserve because he loved her and she had asked. It was impossible not to reach out in return. "I will never find this easy," she said, and her throat was full of tears. "But I want to try. I want to stay, to–"

She kissed him so he would know how much she meant it. Passionately, frantically, as if she could wipe out the memory of Amaret with her touch.

༄

The room was lost in shadows, the candles reduced to guttering flames which danced countless reflections through a spider web drift of hair. Medair let strands slip through her fingers, and shifted so she could better see Illukar's back, and the blue line which ran down his spine. She had discovered how very sensitive he was there, and traced the line now, down to the small of his back, watching his reaction. He turned to catch her hands.

"We will not sleep at all, if you follow that path," he murmured. She answered this by kissing him until his heart was beating faster, but she knew that tomorrow would be inordinately wearying, so she eventually subsided. It should feel wrong to be so happy, but she did not.

"I am content to keep Avahn as my heir," he said abruptly, and she guessed that, like her, his head was too full of thoughts of the future to let him sleep. After hearing the truth of Amaret's miscarriages, the question of children had become impossibly daunting. The association alone would be soul-destroying, and she desperately wanted to protect him from hurt.

"I would like settle into this role before thinking about taking on another," she said, touching his arm. His skin was velvet-soft.

"It is not an issue." He could not quite manage a reassuring tone. Moving back, Medair looked into his eyes, at the ghost destroying the contentment of a moment before. This was a part of *his* past which would not rest quietly while she put off thoughts of tomorrow. They couldn't hope to just push it to the back of their minds.

"It is an issue," she told him, her voice shaking. "I'm probably the worst woman in the world for you to love. Because I can't pretend bearing an Ibisian child will not be complicated for me." She shook her head. "But your child, Illukar. I do want that. I am not ready for it, but I want it. Fiercely. I want to spend all my life with you and I want to have children by you." She swallowed any hint of tears, refusing to be so selfish as to cry on him again. "I never find my path a clear one, but I know that I don't want this decision to be made for us by Amaret."

"Then it will not be." His voice was breathy, and he touched her face delicately. A stark acknowledgment that children would never be a non-issue with him, and he was overwhelmingly glad that she did not reject the idea. "When this hunt is over, we will talk of what comes next," he went on. "Children are something we need not embark upon for many years, but I would like to marry you soon, Medair."

"When this is over," she agreed, almost without quaver. Naked in his arms, marriage seemed only a small step further, and she was light-headed in the aftermath of finally giving up chasing her own tail about what was the right path.

"I am still sending you to Athere tomorrow," he added.

"I have a feeling there might be almost as many people in Athere inclined to kill me as there are in Gyrfalcon Castle. Falcon Black." She touched his face, revelling in her freedom to do so, and the pleasure such a tiny act gave them both. "The purists on top of everything else. At least I think I know, now, why Keris las Theomain tried to kill me."

"Because of this." His eyes were grave.

"Because of you. When you sent her to make sure I didn't leave Athere."

He closed his eyes. "I was not unaware that Jedda had ambitions centred on me. If she hid purist sentiment along with that, then it may well be that her ambitions were mixed with the whispers that the Cor-Ibis line should rule because the Saral-Ibis line has been corrupted with Farak-lar heat. Foolishness."

"I see we will make possibly the most unpopular marriage of the century," she said lightly, and then had to grip his hand hard, because all her doubts hadn't gone away just because she was trying not to listen to them.

"Medair–" he began, but she shook her head. It wasn't the moment to air her fears.

"I wonder if and how the purist cause has been changed by the Conflagration," she said. "With the cold blood less...liable to dilution, they might not care so much."

"Difficult to say. Those within the shield wall of Athere have not been changed." He paused. "I do not...I do not know what, in this remade world, became of Amaret. With the reason for her self-destruction altered, did our marriage run a different course? I am not equal to asking Ileaha that."

The wound left by Amaret cut to his core. And Medair doubted she could find any response which did not sound wrong, so she simply pressed closer to him, thankful that she had spoken to Ileaha long enough to be confident that Illukar would not find himself still married. Any remnant of contentment lost, they held each other as if locked arms could keep back all threat of hurt.

Gradually the rigidity of Illukar's muscles eased, until Medair felt he was ready to move through painful territory. "I don't know if I will ever truly grow used to the world being remade," she said. "Let alone the possibility of further changes. I suppose it's unlikely Ileaha's will be the only transformation."

"No." Control regained, Illukar shifted back, and held up a hand, frowning at it. "I have been casting spells which I do not have set, without any preparation, without any incantation at all. A change more subtle than Ileaha's, but quite as profound."

World-shaking. Casting time was an adept's greatest weakness. Without the need to prepare in advance, an adept's effectiveness would be ten-fold. They looked at each other and didn't need to name the implications. Nor was Medair slow to wonder if she, too, had been changed and simply didn't know it.

"I don't yet control it consciously," Illukar went on. "Merely find myself casting some of the simplest spells as if I have never needed to prepare them. Something for me to experiment with, when time permits."

"When we get home," Medair whispered, preferring to focus on another aspect of their shared future. She had meant to move them to a less difficult topic, and she was surprised to see Illukar's eyes darken.

"I don't even know if Finrathlar exists," he said. "Or what form it takes in this new Farakkan." He gathered her closer. "You had to do that, didn't you? Go home, to find out if it was still there and what it looked like?"

"Yes." She struggled against the inevitable plunge of spirit that memory conjured, but succeeded only in worrying herself further. They were not even close to home territory, problems with purists, or the frightening prospect of Medair an Rynstar going so far as to marry an Ibisian. She remembered her strange feeling of certainty regarding Vorclase, and it obligingly revisited her. Vorclase was still in Falcon Black and they would see him yet.

Medair slid out of Illukar's arms, but only so she could cross to lock the door. She blew out the last surviving candles before returning to the bed. He still glowed. If the effect remained, it would never be truly dark when he was there.

"We will find out together," she said, feeling wrong and pleased and sad all at the same time. Out of so many contradictory emotions, all she could do was choose the best one.

TEN

A sharp *tink* startled her awake. The room was full of sunlight and the scent of wood polish. Illukar, warm at her side, lifted himself to one elbow. He was looking at the door, frowning, then he tensed as a key turned in the lock. Their own key, falling to the floor, must have been what woke her. Medair sat up, trying to disentangle herself from Illukar's twining hair. She had no chance to do more before the door opened and Vorclase walked in.

As Medair suppressed a startled gasp, Illukar made a sharp movement with one hand and was suddenly holding a ball of glowing gold. In another moment he would have thrown it, but Vorclase held up a hand and said, with a tolerant air: "Surely you've heard the war is over, Keridahl? I'm not here to attack you. I'm well aware what it would cost Decia if we tried to revenge ourselves."

"Then why are you here?" Illukar asked, his voice colder than Medair had ever heard it. The glowing ball remained steady, and she breathed deeply to try and slow her racing heart. What had happened to the kaschen supposedly guarding their rooms?

"To offer my help," Vorclase said. He seemed to be the same man who had chased her from Bariback. She could see he was wary, beneath an assumption of ease. He kept his hand at a pointed distance from the hilt of his sword. "Or to ask for yours, perhaps. There is something which must be dealt with, and soon."

Medair, reduced to clutching a sheet to her chest, shifted as Vorclase moved away from the door. He looked at her, his expression difficult to read. Someone had told him where they were, and given him a key. Whatever Sendel's decree, they could not simply treat Decians as allies.

"King Xarus left me on guard duty because I failed to retrieve you," Vorclase said. "Medair an Rynstar. I begin to see why you were so adamant against joining us."

"Speak your piece, Captain," Illukar said. Tranquillity was still absent from his voice, and Medair guessed how much he resented the intrusion on their privacy. But he released the golden ball, apparently believing that they were not immediately threatened. "I presume you have not killed our guard?"

"A tap to the head, nothing more," Vorclase said, smoothly. Then he frowned. "You know, of course, of Tarsus. It was he who told me of the King's defeat. He fled here after the battle, if you could call that slaughter a battle, and had lost himself in the catacombs. I found him yesterday, and he told me what had happened." He looked at Medair again. "One side or the other had to die, I suppose."

"That is war." Her voice was steady. She had made her choice, and would live by it. Or at least try to deal with it without breaking down every time the subject was raised.

"It was decisive, at any rate." Vorclase sat down on the chair Medair had used the night before. "Does it count as blood on your hands, or on Farak's?"

"I think you had better return to the subject of Tarsus," Medair said, tightly. He was alive, then, the supposed descendent of Grevain Corminevar's eldest son. The discovery made her feel tight and panicked, and her stomach fluttered.

"Yes, so do I." Vorclase's gaze shifted over her shoulder to Illukar. "I want immunity for him, Keridahl. Your word that he will not be killed, that he will be allowed to go to asylum in the West."

"I am intrigued to know why you come to me with this," Illukar said. He sounded concerned now, not angry. For Vorclase, who was obviously no friend of Sendel's, not to take the opportunity to flee suggested a major problem. "He has the gate device, doesn't he?"

"You've always had a way of seeing to the heart of an issue, Keridahl." Vorclase did not quite hide a savage bitterness, but the problem at hand was evidently more important than old enmity.

"It's destroying him. He broke it somehow, getting back here, and it–" He shook his head. "He is truly the heir, Keridahl. There was no trickery. And I, for my sins, am sworn to defend him. I could hardly miss what that thing's doing to him, so I tried to take it from him. Now he's running from me as well and I don't think anyone but an adept can hold him. I can't do it on my own at any rate."

"Tell me more of the device."

"King Xarus conjured the thing. And it did all that he wanted – summoned those gates, took the army to Athere, gave him his chance to strike before Palladium could gather its strength. It looks like a big piece of glass mounted in ebony and now it's cracked. Perhaps he just dropped it; I don't know. Tarsus doesn't seem able to put it down. He clutches it to his chest, trying over and over to get it to transport him out of here."

"And he is in the tunnels beneath Falcon Black?" Illukar had evidently heard enough. He slid out of the bed and collected discarded clothing, paying little attention to Vorclase's sardonic gaze. Medair kept to her sheet. "When did you last see him?"

"Less than a decem ago. I've been chasing him half the night, but he knows the catacombs too well to let me hunt him into a corner, and alone I can't block him off."

"You also know the catacombs?"

"Better than anyone else up here, I'd wager." Vorclase grimaced. "Sendel is not known for her tolerance of me. I trust you'll be able to make her see the importance of rescuing Tarsus over clapping me in chains for not running to let her out of her box."

Illukar ignored him, crossing to the bed to touch Medair's hand. "Will you check on Avahn?" he asked. "And then bring Kel ar Haedrin to the room Queen Sendel was working out of yesterday?"

"Of course," Medair said.

Vorclase watched them derisively, but kept to business. "And your word, Keridahl, that he'll not be harmed? That he'll be given free passage?"

"He will not be harmed," Illukar said. With two practiced loops, he gathered his streaming hair into a loose tail. "His freedom is another question. It can be settled after we have him in hand."

"He's not a pigeon, Keridahl." Vorclase followed Illukar to the door, then glanced back at Medair. His mouth twisted, and he shook his head. Then they were gone.

ॐ

"Medair." Avahn attempted a smile. His eyes were swollen into slits and his voice was a hoarse fragment, but he was conscious, propped up against a mound of pillows. Ileaha, who had opened the door for Medair, nodded briefly and left, her face particularly blank.

"I can't really say you're looking better, Avahn," Medair said, settling onto a chair by his bed. She felt quietly relieved by his alert, if fragile air.

"Can't say I feel any better," he croaked, and then took a couple of deep breaths, imperfectly hiding his distress at his own weakness. "Physician says lung never same. Keeps telling me not talk," he added with a stubborn grimace, and looked at the door.

"It's good advice. Listen instead." She told him what Vorclase had revealed. "It explains a lot. Why we arrived in the forest, why the castle guards didn't seem to be looking for us."

"Trust Vorclase far as throw him," Avahn griped, then shook his head. "Not true. Plays by rules, just different ones. How soon?"

"Right away, I expect. You, however, can look forward to an attempt from Athere to open a gate here."

"Won't happen." Avahn shrugged feebly. "Changed too much. Enjoy Decian hospitality." A strange expression flickered across his face and he fell silent. Medair watched him, knowing that she couldn't just sit here and not tell him that she had agreed to marry his cousin. He would be the first person she should tell, and perhaps the most important. She wasn't altogether certain how to go about it.

"Have you grown very used to being Illukar's heir, Avahn?" she asked, awkwardly.

To her surprise, Avahn immediately crowed with delight, then fell into a fit of painful coughing. It took a glass of water to settle him, but he smiled all the while and wheezed, immediately he was able: "Accepted him? Knew something there. Care less about being heir."

Medair tried to control her conflicting expressions, then shook her head, passing over agony and exasperation both. "You would have made an excellent Keridahl, Avahn."

"Bosh," Avahn said, succinctly. "Congratulations, Medair. Happy for you both."

"Thank you." She was going to cry if she wasn't careful. But it felt good.

"Recruit you for match-making," Avahn added, looking at the door again. A frown further distorted his swollen, ravaged face. New emotions touched his voice: longing, uncertainty. Ardent desire. "Bad timing. Not at best."

"No." He certainly wasn't, but Medair couldn't help but be pleased that Avahn was apparently ready to reach out to Ileaha.

"Won't even tell me her name," he added, with an edge of frustration, and Medair's heart sank. "Wasn't with us after gate. Velvet Sword?"

"Yes, I rather think she is."

"Doesn't like me much. Or not. When I woke, the *look* in her eyes!" He coughed again, waved away water. "Always told too rash – but I mean to have her."

"Did you actually *look* at her?" Medair asked. "Listen to her voice? You must have–"

"Must what?" Avahn asked, catching her distress. He tried to sit up and she hastily pressed him back down. "What is it?"

"Oh, Avahn." Medair shook her head, not knowing where to start. Gravely injured, he had opened his eyes to see a beautiful stranger, her face suffused with the love Ileaha had hidden so long. And he had fallen, tumbled into passion, whether true or fleeting. Shown his desire to an Ileaha he thought was a stranger, because her Ibisian blood was now dominant. Medair could hardly picture a worse misstep.

"She's promised, isn't she? Or *var-ma*? But she looked at me, like, like–" He began to cough again, helplessly. For a moment it seemed he was on the verge of another fit, but gradually he regained control. His breathing moved from ragged to shallow, and he was able to drink water. She sat by his bed, watching him until, finally, he turned his head to look at her again.

"What, then?" The coughing had reduced his voice to the barest whisper. "Who is she?"

❧

"Ileaha."

Medair had found Ileaha behind the sixth door she opened. She was standing by a window overlooking the eastern forest. Tall, slender, with that straight, perfect braid only a breath from sweeping the floor. She could be a portrait of a model Ibisian, but for the taut anguish in her stance.

"I told him," Medair said softly, when Ileaha didn't turn from the window.

"And was he much dismayed?" The north wind could have spoken.

Thinking on Avahn's horrified reaction, Medair nodded. A futile gesture, when Ileaha's gaze was fixed so rigidly on the forest outside.

"Even Illukar did not recognise you at first, Ileaha," she said. "I certainly didn't, and I'm not injured."

"You did not try to quote one of Telsen's love sonnets at me either," Ileaha replied, and the bitterness in her voice could have blighted generations. Medair closed her eyes.

"There is little I can say to that," she said, searching for something which would not make it worse. "I can't blame Avahn for responding to what he saw in your face, but he has scant excuse for never having looked before."

"Not till I was this." Ileaha gestured at herself, the coiled intensity of the movement reminding Medair horribly of when she had leapt across the bed to kill Jedda las Theomain. Moving to her side, Medair saw that her eyes were fixed on nothing.

"There was never a moment of desire, before. Avahn might pretend to care little for his role, play feckless, heedless, eschew the demands of his role, but he is as traditional at his core as any of the blood. He would never consider a half-breed."

Savage. But was she right? Avahn had certainly been inclined to mock Ileaha, had shown a disdain which might have been due to her mixed heritage. But he had not been the least bit perturbed by the prospect of a child of Illukar and Medair's succeeding the Dahlein, and his taunts has revolved around Ileaha's 'lack of spine'. "You never showed yourself to him, either," Medair said, quietly.

"Don't pretend that he has been hiding forlorn hopes about me," Ileaha spat back. She was practically vibrating with tension.

"I'm not. He said–" Medair hesitated, terribly afraid of making things worse. She had been Herald, not diplomat. But Ileaha seemed to be on the verge of doing something truly drastic. "He said that it had never even occurred to him."

"No. Not a yellow-haired pauper. Not warm blood."

"Not, according to him, 'until I woke out of a nightmare and saw a woman who looked on me as if I were the dawn after a thousand year night'," Medair said, taking excruciating care, just as Avahn had.

Ileaha's pale brows drew together. "Fine words," she said, scathingly.

"But quite true."

For a breath or two, it seemed that Ileaha would listen. Then, tormented beyond endurance, she recoiled. A knife, glass-sharp, appeared in one hand and she caught up that long tail of white hair with the other. Before Medair could so much as gasp, she had sawn off the braid as close to her scalp as possible, leaving herself a ragged, abbreviated bob. The nape of her neck looked painfully exposed.

"Don't!" Medair protested inadequately, and earned herself a defiant, frantic glance as Ileaha flung the braid out the window. It twisted in the air like a living creature, then fell to the rocks below.

ELEVEN

ince Ileaha had not returned to Avahn's room, Medair asked Kel ar Haedrin to watch over him, and headed down the corridor to the central dining hall which Queen Sendel had adopted as her base of operations in apparent preference to her brother's throne room. Tarsus' survival was a double-edged gift. Medair could not be anything but glad not to have killed him, but she could not pretend that his death would not have made what came next less complicated.

There was no way to be certain how much difference the Conflagration had made to the question of his descent. He might be no more a direct heir of Emperor Grevain than N'Taive was a Mersian Herald, but the past she remembered made no difference to the facts of a remade world. She would–

A hand over her mouth.

An arm swiftly followed, clamping across her chest, pulling her back, and someone came from one side, bending to grab and lift her legs. Surprise froze Medair only for a moment, and then she writhed, twisting in their hold. She bit the hand, or tried to, because there were allies in the rooms ahead and behind and all she had to do was call out–

Movement. They were carrying her away, and she fought harder, furiously now because she would not die here, not now, not when at last it had seemed possible to live.

"We just want to ask you a question!" hissed a voice, young, choked.

Medair still fought, because she did not dare trust, and succeeded in wrenching her face free as they came near to tumbling down a short flight of stairs. She drew breath to shriek, but one of her captors slapped her, hard enough to snap her head to one side, and then there was a door, closing behind them and suddenly she was free, dumped unceremoniously on a flagged floor before a banked fire.

Gulping air, she assembled her limbs, drawing herself together in case it was necessary to fight, but her captors were backing away, and Medair was able to calm herself enough to measure what she faced.

A kitchen. Large, clean, with two entrances, both shut. A gangling boy blocked the one they'd entered through, and a pregnant woman holding a fire-iron rested her back against the other. A younger boy, of perhaps ten years, stood in the centre of the room next to a girl five or so years his senior, and an older woman seated in a chair.

Not an immediate attack. Medair considered her chances of forcing her way through one of the doors, but since they hadn't attacked her, she would catch her breath and wait, at least until her ears stopped ringing. The slap had been hard.

"What question?" she asked, wondering if it would be 'why', and knowing her reasons could no more satisfy these people than Ieskar's had been adequate for her.

"Is it true that there's no survivors?" It was the pregnant woman who asked, voice sharp.

"No." She saw the change wrought in them by that single word, and regretted giving false hope. "I heard that a handful survived. Those who had no weapons, or threw them down. But it was only the smallest number."

"Kerika would never give up her sword," the young boy said, and then ducked his head down, hands balling into fists. "Never."

"But what killed them?" The pregnant woman again. She was at no pains to hide her anger, an obvious desire to lash out. "Palladium was unready, outnumbered. Whatever foul arts the White Snakes could have used, they could not, should not – it must be some kind of trickery. I don't believe you. The battle is still being fought, and you're just lying to protect your hides."

"It was the Horn of Farak." Medair paused, struggling to find the words, then told them the thing she had to: "Medair an Rynstar used the Horn of Farak, and...and Farak answered."

It was like she had slapped them. They gaped: stunned, betrayed.

"But *why*?" The stripling girl this time, stepping forward not in anger but entreaty. "Why would Farak do that?"

That was not how Medair had been looking at the issue at all, and she had no immediate answer.

"Now I know you're lying," the pregnant woman said. "If Medair an Rynstar has truly been reborn, then the White Snakes would be gone, lost. She searched for the Horn of Farak to *kill* them."

"She searched for the Horn of Farak to protect Athere," Medair said. "And did."

"We went to *free* Athere!" The words were shouted and the woman started forward, raising the fire-iron as if it could give lie to Medair's answer.

"Let be, Tercia."

The older woman sagged in her chair as the skin sagged on her bones, but her voice held command.

"Did you see it?" she asked Medair. "Will you swear it, on Farak's name, that what you say is true? It was the Horn of Farak which lost us this war?"

"I swear it, by Farak's Grace."

"And so." The older woman shook her head. "Without Farak's favour, there was never any hope of victory."

"I still don't see why," the stripling girl said. "Why would Farak turn her face from us?"

"I can't speak for – I don't know," Medair said. "Perhaps Farak would have answered any who used the Horn."

"And the Herald? Our cause was just. Tarsus, he is the direct heir of the last Emperor. It makes no sense, that Medair an Rynstar would use the Horn against him."

"To save Atherians. To save someone else who is also a direct heir of the last Emperor. To–" Medair sighed, because she knew that nothing she could say was going to ease their grief, or soothe their hatred. "In the end, perhaps merely because more people would have died if the battle was brought to the streets. I'm sorry.

I wish I could do more, I wish I could tell you something that would make it better, but words will not bring back the dead. Or dull your loss."

Any response was lost as the door behind the older boy was thrust open, catapulting him forward. He yelled as he fell, and the pregnant woman stepped forward, raising her fire-iron, only to meet Ileaha's sword. Medair started to cry out, but should have trusted Ileaha, who was abruptly holding both sword and fire-iron, and had retreated a step, flanking Islantar, who walked into the kitchen with as much dignity and calm as he would approach a room full of allies. His eyes sought Medair and he nodded, the tiniest motion.

"Keris," he said. "I am glad to find you."

"Kierash," Medair said.

Islantar had turned his attention to the small collection of Decians, and perhaps his inherent gravity would have kept them silent even if Ileaha had not been at his side, for all that he was a hated White Snake, invading the place which was their home.

"Between us there is a gulf I do not think it is possible for me cross," he said. "Not today. I do not ask it, only give to you my profound sorrow."

He bowed, a simple, but deep gesture, and turned without a word, and Ileaha and Medair followed, and closed the door behind them.

"I am sorry, Medair," Ileaha said. "I should not have left you."

Medair shook her head, then looked at Islantar. "I couldn't tell them who I was. I couldn't admit it."

"You couldn't tell them who you were because they would have killed you," he said, pragmatically, but his voice changed as he continued. "And then we – I do not quite know how we would have reacted. What gain, what good, to strike them down? But this is one incident and there will be others, death for death. A snowball tumbling down a hill, collecting more and more grievous injuries, weighed down by every slight and every retaliation."

And Islantar tasked by Grevain Corminevar – or Farak herself – to heal Palladium would not achieve that by ignoring Decia's wounds.

"I'm glad I spoke to them," Medair said. "It won't make them hate me any less, but at least they won't have to wonder why."

She let out a long breath, and realised she was shaking. But still alive, able to take another step. Fumbling her way forward.

"I miss believing I was right," she added, but too softly for them to hear.

TWELVE

Illukar and Vorclase stood in temporary alliance before Queen Sendel. Medair very much wanted to talk to Illukar about Avahn and Ileaha, but had to content herself with joining the group standing before the long table which had been thrust to the back of the dining hall. Questions of retaliation, let alone broken friendships, were nothing to wild magic. The problem of Tarsus was paramount, and there was no sign of a search party being formed.

"I should be able to sense it," Illukar was saying. "That is what concerns me most. This device summoned and fuelled gates sufficient to transport tens of thousands – a feat beyond the capacity of any group of mages alive. It is an artefact on the level of the Horn of Farak and it should blaze its presence like a small sun. But I cannot sense it at all."

"And what does that mean, precisely?" Queen Sendel asked impatiently, glaring at Vorclase all the while, but willing to hear an explanation.

"That it must draw power from outside itself." Islantar, bracketed by Herald N'Taive and Ileaha, made an expansive gesture at the castle about them. "Wild magic."

Sendel was unimpressed. "Well, I cannot say I'm surprised. Xarus was ever one for the shortest path. You think it dangerous, do you?" They looked at her. "I see that you do. Then we will turn out that rabbit warren once and for all. You may consider yourself under charge, Vorclase, and on recognizance only until Tarsus occupies the next cell."

"Your Majesty." Vorclase bowed neatly, not losing his sardonic edge. "If we can now at last move on to the logistics of the problem?"

"Your deference overwhelms, as usual," Sendel replied, and made a dismissive gesture. "No doubt you have some elaborate scheme?"

He did indeed and, what's more, a finer grasp of Falcon Black's current resources than anyone else they'd encountered. Medair wondered what Sendel would do with him, after everything had settled down. And whether he'd allow it.

"One final point," Illukar said, after Vorclase had finished outlining his plan. "Any writings of King Xarus, and most especially any books of arcane research, must be destroyed untouched and immediately."

"Extravagant," Sendel commented, her eyes narrowing. "And hardly convenient. I am unlikely to be convinced that I must destroy State documents. They will need to be sorted."

"There should be no need to convince you," Illukar replied, quietly. "King Xarus discovered how to summon wild magic, and fashioned this device. Sorting the documents is too great a risk. We can allow no possibility of his knowledge being used by others."

Sendel was in a difficult position, especially if she hoped to convince Palladium not to take control of Decia while it was stripped of defenders. She did not hide her dislike of the situation. "I suppose you would have me destroy every piece of writing in Falcon Black?"

"That would be ideal," Illukar replied, and she snorted.

"I have no doubt. Tell me, Keridahl: do you know how to summon wild magic?"

"No." He said the word crisply, clearly, as a whole thing in itself. His chin lifted just a little and Medair realised he was insulted. But evidently he decided to make allowances, because after a moment he went on. "There are no exemptions." He looked toward Islantar, who inclined his head. "After the Blight," Illukar continued, "all knowledge of illegal magics was purged at every level. No-one is immune to temptation."

Sendel lifted a hand in compromise, although she looked anything but convinced. "Documents in Xarus' warrens will be destroyed, unexamined. For now, his apartments in Falcon Black will be sealed, and we can argue about the disposal of their contents another time. Go find Tarsus, so that we might move on to what is truly important."

Formalising peace. Planning the future. Medair watched as Vorclase began issuing orders, Sendel was claimed by a secretary, and Illukar sent Islantar and Ileaha to keep company with Avahn, since news of the device had postponed any attempt at gate-summoning. Then he had a chance to stop and smile at her, touch her hand and make her heart turn over. She was immediately overcome with dread that she might lose him; foreboding quite as strong as her previous conviction about Vorclase.

"I'd like to come with you," she said, trying to keep sudden dread from her face.

Illukar obviously sensed her unease, and glanced thoughtfully across the room to where Vorclase was instructing the few guardsmen left in Castle Black. "Do you feel he plans some sort of trap?" he asked, leading her into the next room, where a sparse meal had been set.

"Not yet. Though he seems anxious to preserve Tarsus." Medair did not feel equal to trying to explain what had prompted her request, and looked down unhappily.

"Stay close to me, then," Illukar said, not pressing her.

Vorclase was back with them before she had a chance to do more than outline her worry about Avahn and Ileaha. The Decian Captain spread a detailed map on the table and let them study it while he chewed on a fruit-studded bun. There were far more lines than Medair had expected, and she was distracted both by her inexplicable fear for Illukar, and by Vorclase. He was an uncomfortable ally.

"I've only marked the main routes," Vorclase said, keeping a businesslike tone. "Snares are circled and in the corridors you'll see three score marks near the ceiling. Stay to the left, and you should avoid setting them off. I haven't bothered noting the alarms – there's no-one left to warn." His eyes flicked briefly to Medair.

"Where did you last see Tarsus?" Illukar asked, and Vorclase indicated the rough centre of the middle layer. There was the outline of a small room.

"You'll be wanting to fire this place anyway, if you really do plan to torch everything worth reading. There's half a dozen exits from it, and I'm only sure of the one he didn't go down, which leads back to the southern stair. We'll work on the assumption that he's still in this area, block off these points and drive him into here." An unbroken stretch of looping corridor. "Then it will be up to you, Keridahl. Hold him still, knock him unconscious, do whatever it takes to get that thing off him without hurting him."

"Is Tarsus a mage?"

"No. Wanted to be, didn't have the talent." Vorclase stood up, restive, and collected his map. "Let's get this over with."

⊘⊘

"And how long has this little affair of yours been going on?"

Medair glanced at Illukar, who stood a short way back from the line of men blocking the tunnel, engrossed in preparing a set-spell. There was no sign that he'd heard, that he had concentration to spare for listening. Kel ar Haedrin had. Medair could tell from the way the Velvet Sword had shifted her stance.

She turned to look at Vorclase, whose mouth was twisted into a cynical line. This would be only the first of many such enquiries, and not by any means the most contemptuous.

"One day," she replied, with quiet dignity.

His eyes narrowed. "A celebratory fling? Can you truly be Medair an Rynstar? Herald of the Empire? Grevain Corminevar's Voice?"

"I am Medair," she said, feeling primarily sad. "I am no longer Herald. There is no Empire. Grevain died centuries ago."

"At White Snake hands."

"So I'm told." She shook her head. "Save your breath, Captain. I don't need to justify myself to you." Nor did she want to try. It had taken her too long to reach this point as it was.

The look he gave her then reminded Medair forcibly of her location: deep under Falcon Black with two Decian guards for escort. "You consider yourself above reproach? What of Tarsus?

You didn't so much as attempt to discover the truth of his story. Why was that? What happened to all this 'not taking sides' guff you were spouting in Finrathlar? Lasted until the Lord High here gave you a come-hither look?"

"It lasted until Athere was attacked."

"And then you decided a White Snake sat the throne better than your Emperor's rightful heir. And killed half Decia. And you think you can convince me that was the right thing to do?"

"No." Medair sighed, then looked away as Illukar moved, lowering his hands. His face was that particularly expressionless mask which he wore when he was withholding all opinion. "I'm not trying to convince you that it was the right decision, because it wasn't; not for Decia." Her voice wavered and she took a calming breath, her eyes on the guard standing behind Illukar, who made no effort to hide his hatred. "It was right for Palladium, however. It's taken me a long time to accept that Ibisians aren't my enemy any more, that my war is long over. Your war is over now, Captain."

"Forgive and forget? It doesn't work that way, *Herald*."

"I know." She couldn't begin to explain her struggle to rise above her own hatred.

Vorclase shook his head, and turned his attention back to the tunnel along which, if all went to plan, the heir to a dead Empire would soon be driven. Illukar's fingers brushed the back of Medair's hand and she tried to smile at him. A day was a very short time to have been together, and she wanted to touch and talk to him about things which had nothing to do with war. Constrained by the importance of their mission and the antipathy of the Decians, all she could do was stand at his side and wait for Tarsus.

After only a short eternity, she heard the scrape of a boot on stone, the sound of panting breath, and there he was. He staggered to a stop, arms full of faintly glowing glass, and stared at the people who blocked his way.

No-one had mentioned how young Tarsus was: not more than sixteen years, with curling dark hair, a smudged face and a jutting chin. With that jaw, he could well be of Grevain Corminevar's blood, though the resemblance was not otherwise remarkable. And he was terrified, teetering on the verge of both hysteria and exhaustion.

Eyes wide, he whirled, only to find the guards who had pursued him approaching, swords drawn. For a moment it looked like he would try to run through them. Then he took a deep breath, visibly pulling himself together, and pivoted on his heel. His dark eyes found Vorclase's.

"I would never have believed that you would stand at the side of a White Snake, Jan," he said. A Decian accent, and a careful way of speaking which was apparent despite his ragged breathlessness.

Vorclase looked briefly wry, not unaware of ironic repetition. "So I can read the lay of the land," he said, unexpectedly gruff, and Medair realised that he cared for this boy. "War's over; we lost. Sendel will scuffle about trying to keep the country out of Palladian hands. And you're still alive. I want to keep you that way."

"By handing me to a White Snake?" The boy shook his head, grieved. "You are trusting, Jan."

"Desperate." Vorclase broke the line, stepping forward with a hand held out. "I'll do what I don't like if the result's worth the effort. Put that thing down, lad. Don't you see what it's doing to you?"

Tarsus glanced down at the heavy piece of glass he held against his chest. The size of a dinner plate, with a frame of dark wood, it seemed relatively innocuous until he clutched it closer and it sank through cloth and flesh to give them a brief glimpse of pink and white and something which fluttered and pulsed. The sight didn't seem to faze the youth; he simply moved it out of his chest, then tightened his fingers on the frame. Into the frame.

"You're delivering this to them as well," he said, earnestly. His gaze shifted to Illukar, who was standing quietly at Medair's side, and Tarsus looked him up and down with open horror. "A thing of such power, to White Snakes. Jan, you have run mad."

His disbelief was palpable and, as he glanced down at the glass again, a bright shimmer flashed across its surface. That was all that happened, and Medair could barely sense the whisper of power which meant he must have tried to activate it. The effect on Tarsus was more notable: he shuddered and staggered, sweat bringing a slick and waxy sheen to his skin.

Vorclase took the opportunity to take a few more steps forward, but Tarsus backed into the wall as the Captain approached, lifting the heavy glass to chin-level. The Decian guards stirred and Vorclase gestured for them to be still.

"I'll break it," Tarsus said, in a faint, breathless voice. "Get back, Jan, or I'll smash it at your feet."

"Would that be bad?" Vorclase asked Illukar, as he took a reluctant step away.

"It could be disastrous," Illukar replied, then released the set-spell he had prepared. Tarsus flinched away with nowhere to go, and briefly the glass merged with his chest again. And nothing else happened.

Tarsus looked down at himself and smiled with uncertain triumph. "You can't touch me, White Snake!" he said, eyes wide and voice incredulous. "Farak protects her own."

"The device absorbed the casting," Illukar said, glancing at Vorclase.

"Well, that's helpful." Vorclase was disgusted, but spared little of his focus. "Tarsus, we can't stand here all day. Tell me what you want us to do."

"Leave." The young man was collecting himself together again. "Leave me, clear me an exit and give me a horse."

"That's what I'm trying to arrange, boy." Vorclase sounded frustrated. He looked at Illukar. "Better than stalemate."

"The device must remain," Illukar replied, sedately.

"I will *not* give it up! Not to a White Snake!"

"It must be unmade," Illukar said, ignoring the affront in Tarsus' voice. "It is fashioned from wild magic, it draws on wild magic. You, who would rule Palladium, must see the only course open."

The youth looked uncertain, shifting the glass in his arms. "Wild magic?"

"I won't pretend that there are not reasons for Palladium to wish you dead, or at least in custody," Illukar said, blunt and cool.

"Still, you have my word that you may leave, if that is your wish. But not with the device."

Tarsus stared, dark eyes wide. He looked terribly young, hopelessly driven. What had he done, after all, to reach this point? Controlled by Estarion, raised to hate Ibisians, to believe Palladium his by right?

"How can I possibly trust you?" Tarsus asked now, cradling the glass into his chest once again. "You are my enemy."

"I am Illukar Síahn las Cor-Ibis." Illukar said his name as if it was important to fix it in Tarsus' mind. "I have no animus toward you."

Strange how so profoundly Ibisian a speech could have the desired effect. Tarsus was considering it. Medair took a slow breath as he looked from Illukar to Vorclase and back.

"Were you there?" he asked abruptly, his voice high and strained. "At the slaughter?"

"I was on Ahrenrhen Wall," Illukar replied.

"Then I brought you here." Tarsus took a sideways step, toward the middle of the tunnel. "I meant to get the heir, the one called Islantar. You would have bargained for his life, wouldn't you?"

"Certainly."

Tarsus looked down. "He has what is mine," he said, forlornly. "What I would have, now, if the Horn had not sounded." He looked with sudden suspicion at Medair, standing at Illukar's side. "Were you the one who took that from me?" he asked, flatly. "Were you?"

Medair hesitated, aware that Tarsus' anger had returned in full. Denial might be worse than the truth, especially if Vorclase took it into his head to correct her.

"I sounded the Horn of Farak," she said, not wanting it to sound like an admission. This boy had been out there, when the Decian army had been cut down. He had been in the midst of that incredible slaughter, when certain victory had turned into overwhelming defeat. She had killed all who stood with him, who claimed to be fighting for his cause. If he had held a weapon, she would have killed him as well. This boy who might be Corminevar.

For a moment, it looked like Tarsus would simply throw the glass at her. He flushed with furious betrayal, but his disbelief seemed stronger than his anger. "How could you?" he asked, voice breaking. "How could you turn your face from the true Corminevar line to side with White Snakes?"

He pressed the glass so deeply into his chest that Medair could see his spine: a pale, sinuous gleam in a bloody mount. It was a horrible, immensely distracting sight. If he let go of it now, she thought, it would be completely inside his chest. They would have to cut him open to get it out. And she did not want that, did not want this boy to die. True Corminevar or not, there had to be something she could do to alter the course Estarion had set.

"Why do you want the Silver Throne?" she asked, slowly. "Why do you want to rule Palladium?"

The question had confused him. He shifted the glass again and now it was his pulsing heart they watched. How he held the thing at all, she couldn't guess. It was like no artefact she'd ever seen.

"Because it is my birthright," he said. Utter sincerity. True or not, he believed it. And he was as out of place as she was, in the Palladium of today.

"And did you agree with Estarion, that the only way for Palladium to achieve peace is by killing all of Ibisian blood?"

"Yes." Tarsus looked at Illukar briefly and his eyes hardened. "Yes, it's the only way. The rift is too deep, their crime too great."

"How much of Palladium do you think would be left, after that?"

"Enough," Tarsus replied, with only the faintest hint of uncertainty.

"And do you think they'd forgive you?"

"What?"

"You would be the invader, you see." Medair tried to fill her voice with the same inescapable certainty which had kept her from using the Horn a year ago. "You would have killed their friends, wrested the throne by force. No matter how true your bloodline, there is no just path to forcing your way onto Palladium's throne. Five hundred years ago, the cause would be just, but it's too late. That was what I had to accept, when I came to Athere, centuries late. That Palladium is Ibisian now." She couldn't keep the sorrow out of her voice. That fact would always hurt.

"You're wrong," Tarsus said, with a frantic pitch to his words. He backed into the wall again. "There are many in Palladium who would throw the White Snakes down, who would see them crushed into the dirt."

"Yes." Medair looked at him across that gulf of hate. "There are. But why do you think that they're the ones who should choose the present? How more or less right are they than the ones who love the Palladium of today? Why should the will of the ones who can't accept, who dwell in the past instead of living–"

"Stop talking!" Tarsus ran at her, tears streaming down his face, the glass raised as if to strike her down. Everyone moved at once, hoping to wrest the thing from him before he remembered himself and made good his threat to smash it. "You're wrong!" he shouted, as Illukar moved between them. "You're–"

The bloom of power was overwhelming, as like to the Conflagration as anything Medair had experienced. Bright light flashed, and she heard Illukar gasp, then the world dropped out from beneath her feet once again.

THIRTEEN

She was sliding.

In the first moment Medair was completely disoriented, as she fell down a steep, rocky slope. She seemed to be underneath some sort of huge overhang, for she could see hills and blue sky to either side of her but only blackness above and shadow beneath. Around her she could hear men's startled voices, almost entirely drowned by a massive grinding and an explosive fracturing of rock.

Struggling to control her descent, Medair bounced and somersaulted, catching glimpses of flood-lands to her right and a city to her left. She realised she was tumbling into the saddle between two hills and her startled mind struggled to translate the noise which so deafened her. It was from the stony roof above, as it ponderously followed her down the slope.

In the next few moments, panic fired her to heroic efforts, but she couldn't get upright, and found herself heading directly into the centre of the saddle. The great slab of rock above was night falling in the most tangible way, and it was closing the distance, pummelling her with volleys of shattered stone. Frantically she struggled to change her course. She had to get out from beneath before it ground her into paste, but it seemed to stretch for miles in all directions. There was no way.

In the moment after that, a hand caught at her arm. Illukar, typically upright, pulled her almost to her feet. He hurled them both left, out of her tumbling course, and together they half-ran, but mostly fell, down a chute full of dust and a rebounding hail of rocks toward a rapidly narrowing line of sunlight. Medair's lungs were full of sand and her veins thick with acid mud and she couldn't see, could scarcely think, but she knew when they slid out from the shadow of that mammoth weight. She could feel Illukar's hand still tight in hers as she fell some ten or fifteen feet to a slippery slope of grass with mercifully few rocks to bruise them during another tumbling slide. Behind and above them came a thooming clap of thunder, the death-knell of a mountain, and then something which was only silence in comparison. Dust and small rocks sifted liberally over them as they slid into a soft bed of clover and were still.

ॐ

Medair knew she was alive because she hurt. She had a great many sources of pain to consider, though only her left arm came close to unbearable. Scratches, bruises, bumps and grazes and one broken bone. Her head spun and her chest seemed resolved to disown her. The world around her was dust-blurred and distant and her ears were clogged with dirt.

Letting go of Illukar long enough to scrub at her face, she gazed through tearing eyes at a handful of goats fleeing in utter panic down toward the city. And then she did not know what to stare at first, because before her was Finrathlar and above her was Falcon Black.

Her view was blocked as Illukar snatched her to his chest. She could hear his heart thundering at a full-out gallop, and with her one good arm squeezed him painfully back, thanking Farak for his survival. Her disbelief was reflected in his face.

She had never imagined Illukar in such utter disarray; the cuts and grazes and fine coating of dust were nothing compared to the incredulity in those wide grey eyes. Not even Ibisian reserve was proof against someone moving mountains.

But he was recovering, enough to discover her forearm, with a bone protruding in a most irregular fashion and blood oozing liberally over her hand. Moving the arm had been a mistake, and the look on Illukar's face only made it hurt more. Medair blinked rapidly, dots swimming before her eyes. Sucking in a breath, she tried not to mewl at the pain.

"I'll be all right," she said, unconvincingly, managing to get her feet under her. She was shivering, and her legs were rubbery as she stood, but they held her. Wanting to sit right back down, she looked up at Falcon Black properly, and saw that half the hill had come with the castle. It looked as if it had been sliced cleanly across at an angle which did not quite fit the line of the two hills it now rested between. The dust was settling around the transplanted hill and as she watched, the largest of the castle towers shuddered and collapsed, stones bouncing down into the valley bare feet to their right. The entire thing was canted in toward the city, tilted as if set to slide from its precarious perch.

"Can you see anyone else?" Illukar asked, his voice breathless as he searched the rock-studded slopes around them. He put his hands on her shoulders to steady her and she knew she must look on the verge of collapse but at this moment he could not spare his attention from the overriding problem. Not the castle teetering above, but Tarsus. Tarsus and the device.

"No wild magic?" Medair tried to focus on searching the slopes, spotting a demolished chair and a sprinkling of candles among the tumble of rocks, but no people.

"Not now." Illukar had seen someone, and led her carefully left as more small stones bounced down the slope. Every step made her arm feel like it was about to explode, but all she could do was try not to jar it and refuse to break down. "What was summoned was completely consumed by the gate," he continued, looking jerkily up at the castle and then down at Finrathlar. "I cannot feel any residue. It has not broken loose."

Medair blinked at him, trying to focus beyond her arm. He was speaking in small bursts, was still hollow-eyed with shock, and he had not hidden his fear. He was thinking of the Blight, of the inevitable consequence of a malfunctioning device which summoned wild magic in such monstrous proportions. And Finrathlar. His beloved home, the seat of his Dahlein, with a Decian castle perched above it and, somewhere, wild magic which had screamed at them, and then vanished.

"So picturesque, Keridahl."

It was Vorclase, his voice faint and unsteady. He was propped against a rock, one of his legs a splintered mess. The mangled body of a young guard lay within hand's reach.

"How does he do it?" he continued, addressing Medair in what he apparently meant to be a weary drawl. But he could barely get the words out, was grey-faced, dull-eyed and shuddering. "The hill fell on him as well and he stands there looking a little mussed and dusty, while we're all blood and splinters and this poor fellow is so much sausage." He looked at the body, then coughed and gingerly touched the side of his head, as if to make certain it was still there. "Can you see the boy?" he asked, rallying. "I know he's here. I had hold of him, just for a moment, when the whole thing fell out from underneath us."

"Not as yet, Captain." Finding Vorclase seemed to resurrect Illukar's poise. "He will be found."

After another glance up at the looming castle, Medair decided to sit down, and found herself a rock she wasn't likely to fall off. Falcon Black seemed inclined to stay where it was, at least temporarily, and she would rather wait for someone from Finrathlar to come and find them. Dust was filming over the blood coating her hand, and the slow flow was making her light-headed. It seemed likely she had broken a couple of fingers as well, and it was so hard not to howl and moan like a child.

"I'm beginning to see why you were so bent on getting hold of that bit of glass," Vorclase said faintly, as Medair tried to find a way to hold her arm which didn't make the pain worse. "Might not be a problem any more." Then he laughed, a coughing sound which was mostly moan. "I'd give a lot to see Sendel's face."

Illukar didn't reply, busying himself with a casting. Medair recognised the phrases of a wend-whisper and remembered Islantar, somewhere in the castle above. Not in the tower. Their rooms hadn't been in the tower.

"I'm not certain we would know it, if the device was destroyed," she told Vorclase. Given its insubstantial nature, the gate device might be perfectly at ease with a castle sitting on top of it. Since she could not see anyone else moving on the slope, chances were Tarsus was dead.

"He could be on the other side," Vorclase said, following her line of thought. He looked with feverish anger at his leg, evidently the only thing stopping him from scouring the countryside. "If he gets into the Shimmerlan, we might never catch up with him."

"A trace can be established, whether he is under or beyond the castle." Illukar sat down beside Medair, looking as if the movement pained him. "There is surely some personal item in Falcon Black which can be used as a focus."

Vorclase grunted. He was fading, and she had to strain to hear when he spoke. "When he stays in the castle, it's in Westring Tower. You'll find bits of that halfway to your market square." He lifted his hand to gesture at the stone-strewn hillside.

Sparing a glance for the fallen tower, Illukar turned his attention to Medair, tearing a strip of cloth from his demi-robe to tie around her elbow.

"I am not steady enough to attempt to mend this," he said. "But there is certain to be a useful adept in Finrathlar." He looked down at the city again, as if searching for some change. But, so far as Medair could tell, it was Finrathlar exactly as she had last seen it. Peaceful, very Ibisian. No sign of fire, no sign that the flames of the Conflagration had swept over it.

The useful adept soon arrived, in excess. For a moment, it seemed that half of Finrathlar had turned out, with spells at ready and hastily snatched weapons. The sudden appearance of a massive, if crumbling, castle had evidently been interpreted as an attack. Illukar set the first few people who spotted him to searching the immediate area for Tarsus. Then a group of formally dressed Ibisians came striding up the hill, and at the sight of them Illukar's face lightened.

"Sedesten." Sounding positively relieved, he gripped the arm of the person at the fore of the group: a very tall, quite pretty man with eyes an unusually dark shade for an Ibisian. His earrings identified him as Keriden and adept, and every one of his companions wore the silver sigil of adept attainment in their right ear.

"Quite an entrance, 'Lukar," said Sedesten, in a sweet, husky voice. "What do you want done?"

It had never occurred to Medair that Illukar would have friends. He had always seemed so distant in his dealings with others, separate. She watched his face as he summarised the situation, and saw the confidence there. This Sedesten was someone Illukar not only liked: he trusted the man implicitly.

"Have every possible trace-focus picked out of the rubble of the tower," Illukar said, after he had laid bare the situation. "Captain Vorclase may well be able to identify something belonging to Tarsus." He glanced at Vorclase, only to discover the Decian had lapsed into unconsciousness. "To which end, your skills in bone-knitting will be useful. As for Falcon Black, we will discuss methods of stabilisation once it has been evacuated."

As soon as Sedesten turned away to delegate tasks, Illukar began casting another wend-whisper. Medair occupied herself with trying to pick bits of gravel out of the palm of her battered hand, a task so engrossing she started when Sedesten knelt before her.

"First something to dull the pain," he said, nodding a greeting. "Unless you would prefer to be unconscious?"

"No." Medair wasn't planning to let Illukar out of her sight if she could help it. She had not forgotten how his namesake had died.

Sedesten simply inclined his head and began to cast. All sensation in her arm vanished, with a suddenness which left Medair dizzy. She still felt like she was going to faint, and her heart raced, skipping beats with an unnerving lack of predictability, but she might well have had only one arm for all the sensation remaining in her broken limb.

The other hurts of her body stepped forward to claim Medair's attention. She had skinned her knees, and felt like one dusty bruise, but there was nothing so bad as the break. The adept trickled water and a small vial of greenish liquid over her forearm, systematically sluicing away blood and dirt until the area around the protruding bone was clean. Medair looked away, and saw that two other adepts were working on Vorclase. They had a more difficult task, for his leg was broken many times. Even the most skilled of mages would need to work many small miracles to return it to anything close to its former strength.

Tilting her head back, she stared up Falcon Black. There were people moving up there now, a couple of men making an uncertain attempt to descend the shorn entrance ramp. The castle was not tilted so severely as Medair had initially thought: ten or, at most, fifteen degrees. Enough to make moving about awkward, but not deadly perilous. But it was a long way to fall.

Watching the attempted descent allowed Medair to not think about the casting Sedesten was working, and the way he was moving her arm about, for all she could not feel his touch. She was also deliberately not looking at Illukar, just for these few moments. That uncomfortable sense of certainty and dread had not returned, but she was beginning to suspect those moments were a change which had been made to her by the Conflagration, less obvious than Ileaha's appearance, but no less difficult to deal with.

The strength of her qualms made it impossible to keep her fear from her eyes, and so she did not look at him. It had taken so much to reach the point where she could hold him. The idea of him being snatched away was too much.

But if Tarsus released the Blight, she could not think of a single way to stop Illukar sacrificing himself to it, as the first named Illukar las Cor-Ibis had done during the fall of Sar-Ibis. So it was necessary to find Tarsus, quickly, and ensure that the mirror was safely taken from him. She began to catalogue the contents of her satchel, wondering if anything there would fit her purpose, but then she realised that she didn't have it. She didn't even remember where she'd left it.

All that she had been was now truly gone.

It was some time before Medair realised that Sedesten had stopped casting. She looked down and saw that the bone was no longer projecting, though she still had plenty of cuts and grazes. Healing was a difficult, finicky crafting and one best done in stages, because it drained both caster and recipient. Sedesten, oddly, was simply kneeling in front of her, watching her face.

"Thank you, Keriden," she said, disconcerted.

"The bone will be weak still." He touched one side of the half-closed hole in her arm, not shifting his gaze. "After a thorough cleaning, you should have it and the fingers strapped." Then he added, with a delicate but completely un-Ibisian forthrightness: "I have eyes enough to see that my lord and friend counts your every breath. Take care of him."

He was climbing to his feet before Medair could react. She watched blankly as he picked his way across the hillside to where Illukar stood. They both glanced at her, but were caught up with queries from a dozen sources. The hillside was now swarming with helpers.

Medair watched as Illukar extricated himself and returned to her. He was wearing that customary non-committal expression, and gave no sign of counting anyone's breath. Sedesten must know him well indeed, or was guessing wildly. His words had been a gesture of approval, she thought, and wondered how many in Finrathlar would be glad to see their Keridahl happy, and how many would feel as Jedda las Theomain had.

"Islantar will be down soon," Illukar said, sitting decorously on the rock beside hers. "With Avahn and Queen Sendel. The descent should not be dangerous."

"And Tarsus?"

"No sign. Riders have been sent to search, but this place called the Shimmerlan now abuts the border. I am told it would be possible for Tarsus to have reached the water already. This branch of the Shimmerlan is apparently a marshy place, all islets and reed beds. He could go a long way without a boat."

The sprawling lake which had replaced Farakkan's five central kingdoms was something Medair could still scarcely credit. The kingdom of her birth, her mother's property, all under water. There would never be a time she could let herself think of that.

"But he had a hill fall on top of him, just like us," she pointed out, grimacing at her arm. "After a night with little sleep. He was exhausted." She shook her head at the idea of anyone making any kind of escape after what they'd just been through. "Do you think he knows this lake country? I can't think of any reason for him to transport us to Finrathlar."

Illukar looked up at the looming castle. "I am the cause of this, not Tarsus," he said, the faintest hint of exasperation rising through the bald admission. "Or both of us together, for we were both touching the device. He does not have the reserve of arcane power the device seems to need, like the spark for a fire. That came from me, though the will to leave was his. The destination was most definitely mine."

"Does that mean we need not be concerned with wild magic?" she asked, sitting up straighter. "That he could not unleash the Blight, no matter what he tried to do with it?"

"I do not know, Medair." Illukar's face was a blank mask again. "The device is very unstable. We cannot trust to chance."

They were distracted by a murmur from the crowd, and Medair saw that the first of Falcon Black's occupants were making their way down the slopes. They were holding onto ropes for balance, but the path seemed safe enough after the initial drop from the end of the entry ramp. Sendel was in the forefront, and quickly spotted Illukar, who had risen to his feet. Medair stayed on her rock, not quite certain she was steady enough to stand.

The Decian Queen didn't return Illukar's gesture of greeting. "This is the work of Xarus' device?" she asked, tersely.

"Yes. Tarsus is still unaccounted for."

"Then 'how and why' are of less importance than 'what next'," Sendel said, still curt. Hardly pleased to have her castle transplanted. "I will leave searching for the boy to you, but those in my command are at your disposal in seeing to Falcon Black." She gave the castle one expansive glance. "It seems unlikely to fall now, but I would have it preserved, no matter its location."

Illukar inclined his head, then his gaze went past Sendel to Islantar, leading Ileaha, Kel ar Haedrin and the two kaschen, who each had a corner of a blanket serving as a stretcher for an unconscious Avahn. Herald N'Taive followed at the rear.

Islantar was carrying Medair's satchel. He handed it to her wordlessly, and she looked down at the familiar leather, which she had once been so proud to carry. It was as if it was fated to always return to her, as if it was impossible to leave it behind.

leaha had fallen asleep cradling Avahn's head on her lap. Even dozing she managed to steady him against the jerking of the carriage, and it was typical of the young woman that, no matter how furious she had been, she was still taking every care for his safety. Medair and Islantar shared the opposite seat, packed off to the Cor-Ibis manor, The Avenue, as soon as a carriage could be procured. Illukar had promised to follow soon after, and Medair had gone without demur, not willing to distract him from organising the search for Tarsus. But good sense would not stop her from silently fretting.

"Twenty years. Perhaps thirty. The south will regain its strength, and we will do this again."

Adjusting her numb arm, Medair looked at Islantar. There was a small graze on his chin, suggestive of a fall, but his mouth was firm. Medair was not certain how cloistered the Kierash's existence had been, but she had seen enough dismay in the eyes of those who recognised him to guess how completely out of his experience these extraordinary circumstances must be. Yet he was already looking to the future.

"Do you think it that inevitable?" she asked. "Given Sendel's geas?"

"At least likely. And there are those who will argue that it would be wiser, safer, to annex Decia, make it part of the Palladian Empire once again." Islantar was watching her reaction, as if he thought he could gauge the mood of Farakkan from her face. "And perhaps it would dull the weapons of those who wish to keep wounds open. Perhaps make it more difficult for an organised force to be massed."

"I don't have your answers, Kierash," Medair said. In the aftermath of her fall, it was all she could do to keep a peevish snap out of her voice.

"And are in no mood to find them?" The look he gave her was all Emperor, the sort of survey Grevain would turn on those who offered excuses instead of action. Medair struggled against a sense of injury, thinking him unfair to be pushing her now. But the thought of Grevain stiffened her back, reminding her that she had abandoned the pretence of being an outsider uninvolved in the problems of the present.

"Do you think that question so urgent, then?" she asked. "Above Tarsus and wild magic and a castle threatening to fall on our heads?"

"It is the one urgent to me," Islantar replied, shifting back from Emperor to boy. A grave, serious youth willing to shoulder his burdens – and wanting to focus on anything but the possible price of wild magic. "The disease, rather than the symptoms." He smiled at her apologetically. "You are suffering, I know, and I should not press you, but possibly you do not understand how important you are to what I strive to see. Of all I have known, you have the greatest cause to hate the Ibis-lar as invaders. You experienced the loss of the Empire, you were its Herald. You lived what Estarion and the Medarists and the Hand all try to revive. Yet you set it aside, and used the Horn to defend Athere. If you can heal that wound, how can they not?"

Medair shook her head. "You don't understand, Kierash. I'm no more healed than they. I've merely seen my way to choosing not to mire myself in acts too old to change. But there is no forgiveness in me, not for the invasion."

The words fell from her lips as if it wasn't she who formed them. Something had stepped into the light as she spoke, and she could neither look at it nor hide from it, only feel its anger. It stood stony and uncooperative at the back of her heart; that part which would not stop hating. Did she really think to start a life with Illukar while it lurked there? But she had neither the will nor energy to try and understand it, to attempt to face it.

Her words had quelled Islantar a little, and she felt immediately sorry for him, sitting so alone on the far end of the seat, trying to shoulder the burdens of a kingdom. But he was not easily defeated.

"How then did you make that choice?" he asked. "For that is certainly more than the Hand or Estarion have managed. It is not something which came easily to you, I think."

"No. It did not. Does not. Will not." Medair flinched away from her memories of the previous year. She had certainly not been able to deal with the chasm between past and present when she had first discovered her five hundred year delay. "I didn't want to accept reality and I worked very hard not to. But by the time of Estarion's attack, I had seen too much to continue telling myself that this wasn't my war."

"What changed?" Islantar asked, watching her fixedly.

Medair shook her head sadly. "It was what had not changed, Kierash," she said. "For all I saw of Avahn and Ileaha, for all I came to feel for Illukar, I gave your mother the Horn of Farak because I was still sworn to defend Athere. I forced myself to keep to the letter of my oath, despite the part of me which did not object to Ibisians being thrown down, because if I did not then *my* people, Farak-lar, would have been killed."

"Will you always think of us as White Snakes, then?" Such a quiet question.

"How can I answer that?" she said. "The anger is not always there. When it rises I press it down, and give myself more and more reasons not to let it up again."

"Forbearance, rather than forgiveness."

"I suppose so," Medair said. "But Tarsus, who would rule Palladium, cleaves to this idea of cleansing it first. He believes it the right thing to do. The only way."

The carriage jolted around a corner, reminding Medair just how tired and aching she was. Islantar leaned across to steady Avahn, then looked down at his hand. Against custom, though no longer against law, for him to touch.

"Perhaps, for Tarsus to rule, that would be necessary," he said. "I do not know enough of him. Or Prince Thessan, who is in truth the greater threat, since he is Decia's heir. Do you know," he added, those clear eyes widening in faint amazement, "Queen Sendel had left him locked in those cells? She sent someone to let him out, before we came down."

"They don't seem close," Medair commented, as they at last rattled through the gates of The Avenue. "King Xarus' influence, perhaps."

"Perhaps." The Kierash lapsed into thought, and Medair was glad to give up thinking of any futures beyond getting clean and finding somewhere to rest.

⚮

A pair of Illukar's over-efficient servants had taken charge of Medair. They had scrubbed her and bandaged her, poured hot sugary liquid down her throat and treated her much like a two-year child. The petite Farakkian woman who cleaned and salved her grazes acted like she and Medair had met before, and her attitude, beneath the bland mask of service, was not entirely friendly. Uncertainty was stretching Medair's weary nerves, and she was very glad to see Ileaha, who arrived just as Medair was being wrapped in a voluminous robe.

Looking strangely naked without her braid, Ileaha waited a moment for the two women to tie the sash about Medair's waist, then dismissed them from the room.

"Do I know either of those women?" Medair asked, the moment the door to the guestroom had closed behind them.

Ileaha paused for consideration. "You have been to The Avenue before, so it is likely you have at least seen them. Keris Arona is 'Lukar's selvurgeon – one who heals without magic. The other is Lekmet, who is fourth in the House's order of attendants. They exist in both my memories, but I don't know of any connection with you." Ileaha lifted an equivocal hand. "Despite knowing two worlds, I don't have every answer you seek."

"Do you have the answers *you* seek?" Medair asked, then added: "You seem less distressed."

"Less?" Ileaha looked down at herself. She was wearing another variation of what Medair thought of as the uniform of a Velvet Sword – the most abbreviated of demi-robes over workmanlike shirt and trousers. "Seeing Falcon Black above Finrathlar made my own divides seem...petty. I cannot undo what has been done to me, and there is no gain in running from it. I am two halves of a third whole." She shook her head. "I will not waste my energies repining."

"And Avahn?"

Ileaha's face tightened, then she sighed. "I know it wasn't his intention to hurt me, yet he did. But, if I take his current protestations at face value, his fault was only that he saw too late. And...in either life, there was a bond between us. I can't change that either."

"What was he like? The Avahn from this remade world?"

"Much the same." Ileaha paced about Medair, glancing at the tub of water which had not yet been removed from the room. "In both cases, Avahn turned somersaults to avoid winning Illukar's approval. There were many different incidents, but at core he is the same person. It is on an errand of his that I am here."

"Yes?" Medair was surprised. "He's conscious again?"

"He drifts in and out. One of Sedesten's students is tending him, so there is little chance of a further decline." Ileaha found Medair's satchel and picked it up. "He was most insistent I see to you."

Ileaha wouldn't elaborate further, simply leading a weary and reluctant Medair out of her room and up a flight of stairs to the third level of the house, a place she hadn't been before.

"You are not very different, either," Ileaha said, opening a heavy door of near-black wood. "I have been hoping for this in both my memories." She stepped aside to allow Medair to look into the room.

The covering on the bed immediately captured attention. If someone had taken a dozen armfuls of dragonflies and dropped them onto a mossy hill, it would have something of the same effect. Thousands of embroidered insects seethed together in the centre of the spread and dripped down its sides to hover above the floor. They were delicately rendered in pale, shimmering colours, which saved the bed from overwhelming the rest of the room.

A wide, flat bowl of translucent porcelain, beautiful for the extreme perfection of its proportions, was set upon a black table to her left. It was filled with water, with a scattering of rose petals on the still surface. White screens were set before sun-filled doors of glass, each panel glowing with light so that every fleck in the material was clearly outlined. Two pens had been placed neatly on a block of heavy paper sitting in the exact centre of an ebony writing desk. The room was spare and balanced and inexpressibly Illukar, in a way which made Medair feel his absence acutely.

Ileaha crossed to the chair before the writing desk and set Medair's satchel in its lap. The movement had an air of confirmation and finality about it, as if Ileaha was declaring a homecoming. Medair walked into the room far less certainly, feeling stupidly shy.

"You are wanting to sleep, I know," Ileaha said, and left her, closing the door firmly. The air of light conspiracy was unexpected, especially when Ileaha had been so furiously wounded that very morning. It felt like decades ago, but the sun was not far past midday.

The depth of Ileaha's hurt, and how much of her apparent recovery was merely brave show, was difficult to judge. Medair had not missed the way she had altered course when speaking of Avahn, and her departure felt abrupt. But it was apparently Avahn who had sent her. Could she believe Ileaha had simply chosen to accept and move on? The very thing Medair had struggled so long to achieve. She supposed the important thing was to make the attempt.

Too tired to speculate further, Medair crossed to the bed and sat down. She felt out of place, but pushed the uneasiness aside. Sleep would dull the edge of some of her doubts, and if she was to find any way to help, to think of some solution, she needed rest to clear her mind.

ॐ

There were tiny blue smudges on the very outer edges of Illukar's eyelids. Medair lay staring at them, trying to remember if they had always been there. They might be a symptom of fatigue, or something every Ibisian had, and she had never noticed because she'd never before had the occasion or the desire to study the details of a sleeping Ibisian's face.

It was still the same afternoon, though the angle of the sunlight suggested it was closing in on evening. She'd woken listening to his steady breathing and found him lying next to her, arranged on his side in a position loosely symmetrical to her own. The scratch down his cheek looked older, though it would be a long time before it faded completely. He was dressed in linen, as if he had meant to go out and only stopped for a short rest which weariness had prolonged. That mass of pale hair shone in two neat braids, and he smelled very clean. Quite captivating.

Medair was taking the opportunity to enjoy him, to examine each quirk of his delicate brows and pale lashes, and these little smudges which she'd never looked hard enough to notice before. He was such a beautiful man, and she supposed that was part of the reason she had been drawn to him, along with his intelligence and fine sense of courtesy. But she had fallen in love with him for his smile, and most especially for the tale he had told her of Ourvette's Lake, because he had found his own family's pride amusing.

It was hard to resist touching him, but Medair scarcely let herself breathe in case he woke up and felt he must immediately go take up the reins of his Dahlein. It was a soap bubble moment.

On cue, he opened his eyes. Clear grey, with a scattering of darker crystal flecks. She was glad he didn't sit up immediately, but lay looking back at her. He shifted his hand, so his fingers just touched her splinted ones, and his eyelids dropped as if he was overwhelmed by that simple act. The soap bubble didn't break, and they lay there until a whisper of power trickled into the room and Illukar looked away.

"They are attempting to stabilise Falcon Black," he said. "The majority of the task was to be done with stone, and this casting will be to fuse the supports. The first of many, for it is the work of several days. Weeks, perhaps."

He didn't get up, despite the continuing increase of arcane 'noise'. Medair, feeling glad, shifted her fingers so they brushed back against his, and watched his expression change. It meant a very great deal to him that she wanted to touch him.

"And Tarsus?" she asked reluctantly, not certain she wanted to know any answer.

"No sign. The traces have seemed to fix on him, and then dissipate. Likely, the device absorbs them as it did my own casting. The physical searches continue and Sedesten has spoken to a representative of the Shimmerlan's inhabitants to arrange a hunt in their territory."

"What will you do with him, when he's captured?"

Illukar's brows drew together. "His ultimate fate is a matter for the Kier. Even without Estarion to fuel his ambitions, there are too many who would use him to challenge us, or who would appoint themselves champions of his welfare. Impolitic to kill him, imprudent to let him live."

"Would the Kier be...prudent, then?"

His gaze shifted back to their hands, the tips of her fingers still only grazing his. "I have never known the Kier to be unjust," he said, but continued past prevarication. "He warred against us, no matter that Estarion worked the strings. It is possible the Kier might choose to have him executed. But imprisonment is more likely. I expect it will be a country estate: constant guards, little freedom. And for us, a lifetime of denying that he has been disposed of more permanently."

That would be easier to deal with than an execution. Medair sighed softly, wishing that Tarsus had proven to be an obvious charlatan, the painfully greedy kind who would not rouse such conflicting emotions. "I will never be sure if he was truly Corminevar," she said. "Before the Conflagration."

"No."

Medair watched shadows cross Illukar's face, speculating on their meaning. "Finrathlar is very much the same, isn't it?" she said.

"Its proximity to the Shimmerlan seems to be the greatest change," Illukar replied, and she saw that she had guessed correctly. Something about Finrathlar disturbed him.

"What is it?" she asked.

His lashes swept down again, then he closed his eyes briefly. "It is very much the same," he said, and there was a thread of loss in his voice. "I am in the room which I have long called mine, in the city which is my home and my charge. My mother is buried in the grounds of this house. I recognise it all and cannot mark out something which is not as I left it. Yet today my oldest friend spoke of having travelled with me through a place I have never seen, dealing with a race I have never met." He flattened his hand on the bedspread. "Is this my home, or something which merely resembles it? Did the true Finrathlar die in flame? Did Sedesten? Was The Avenue burnt to the ground and a copy erected in its place? Am I trying to save a place which is not even mine? Am I an impostor in my own home?"

Tiny lines had formed on either side of his mouth. He looked as if he were in physical pain.

"You are Illukar," Medair said, slowly. "And–" She hesitated, then covered his hand with hers. His long, slender fingers made hers look stunted. "I think this is not quite your home. The Conflagration seemed to be–" She chewed her lip, trying to decide just what she thought the Conflagration had done. "I don't–" She paused again, uneasily. "If there had been no shield wall around Athere, and we had been altered to Estarion's purpose, I don't know what I would be. Medair, evidently, but would I have been a Medair who, when she blew the Horn of Farak, destroyed defender instead of invader?"

"I do not think that likely," he said, and she smiled at him, but continued even though she did not like where her thoughts were leading.

"Whether the Conflagration truly killed them or not, those who were outside Athere must have experienced the change as death." Medair looked away from those clear eyes. She wasn't saying anything he hadn't already concluded, merely speaking out loud what weighed on his heart. "They would have felt the flames on them, they would have run screaming and been overwhelmed. Is it something other than death, to be reborn the same day in almost exactly the same situation? Those horse-people certainly aren't the people they were before, and nor is Kyledra and all the other lands drowned in the Shimmerlan. Finrathlar looks the same, but it is not. And yet, that doesn't *change* anything."

"No?" Illukar's hand had closed into a fist beneath her fingers.

"No." Already distanced from the modern world, Medair could not react to its alteration in the same way. She felt helpless in face of his hurt, but stumbled on regardless. "You mourn the Sedesten who was, and the home you remember, but the Sedesten who is doesn't stop being Sedesten for having the Shimmerlan incorporated into his memories. He certainly knows *you*. You are as much a part of this world as you were of the one before the Conflagration. I can't tell you not to mourn that terrible day when Finrathlar watched the Conflagration sweep over it, but don't reject what is here in the meantime. This is still your Dahlein and you are still you. It is still Finrathlar and it will always be your home."

She could tell she had not been very convincing. "Just as it was still Athere for you?" he asked, eyes still hooded.

Medair took a deep breath, thinking through the comparison. "Will you feel you are turning your face from the true Finrathlar if you defend this new one?"

That had been closer to the mark. He looked away from their hands and shifted gingerly onto his back. "In a way. Yes. This is not my Finrathlar. My home and my friends and those in my charge died in flame. I cannot just put that aside, even if their death was not precisely final."

It was difficult to imagine Illukar responding as she had: running off to sulk on a mountain because she could not come to terms with what had gone wrong.

"Then don't put it aside," she suggested, feeling his sense of loss more acutely. "Mourn them. Remember them. The important part is to go on." It had taken her far too long to understand that.

He didn't respond, gazing at the ceiling. It wasn't something he was going to come to terms with instantly. She wondered how he would have felt about her, if she'd been outside the wall.

"How is your arm?"

At times he was suspiciously telepathic. "How is your back?" she asked in return, and he lifted one corner of his mouth, acknowledging that there had been a cause for his stiff movement and winces.

"Bruises on bruises," he said. "But if I were to admit to injuries, a glancing blow to my head was my real concern. I had no wish to try and cast anything of moment while suffering concussion, but it seems that the rap inspired nothing more than a headache, and the rest has rid me of that."

"My arm feels exactly as if it was recently broken and healed," she said. "A dull ache, stiff with bandages and cuts and grazes, but no longer the sort of thing to make me want to keel over." She shook her head. "A *castle* fell on us. We're lucky to be alive."

"Yes." He turned his head so he could look again at their hands, hers now under his. Dragonflies hovered beneath their fingers, and Medair was suddenly uneasy. There was something terribly ephemeral about dragonflies, and she wondered just how long his family had used them as an emblem.

"Why did your mother name you Illukar?" she asked, not even trying to keep her fears out of her voice. "It's as good as *asking* for a situation where you are obliged to sacrifice yourself."

"Or asking that I be capable of meeting such challenges," Illukar replied, at his mildest. The clear gaze was serene once again. "My mother believed strongly in tradition, and it is the practice of the Cor-Ibis line to name a male heir Illukar if he is born in the month of the original bearer's death."

"It's the practice of the Cor-Ibis line to not marry Farak-lar," Medair said.

"True. It is fortunate that I am not entirely traditional." The glow in his eyes would reassure any doubting bride, and he touched her cheek tenderly. "Don't fear for me, Medair. The name has been linked to sacrifice merely because of the character of those who have borne it. It is not a death sentence."

"If Tarsus releases the Blight, is there anyone else with the strength to dispel it?"

"Perhaps not. But that is not quite the issue at hand. If the Blight is released, I will not go forth to combat it as my forebear did. I do not know how."

"What?" A giddy feeling fluttered through Medair's chest, something more complicated than surprise.

"There are no records of just what it is Illukar Kohl las Saral-Ibis did to rid Sar-Ibis of the Blight. I have long presumed the process was somehow related to the summoning of wild magic, because it is otherwise an oversight of ludicrous proportions. Very likely it *was* recorded, and then purged in later centuries during one of the drives to destroy all records of the summoning of wild magic. It may have been accidental. Or a deliberate decision, in those first stark days after Sar-Ibis' destruction, not to document even the cure, in case it became the cause. Whatever the truth, it leaves us without a defence now."

"I shouldn't be glad, should I?" Medair said, unsteadily.

"No." He smiled, and touched her face. "Do you think me so anxious to leave you?"

"I think it likely you share the character of other Illukars."

"Perhaps. There will be little choice but to try and stop it, if the Blight is released." He looked at her thoughtfully. "But I am forgetting you, Medair. Was the method of destroying the Blight ever discussed in your presence?"

Medair had been distracted by a possibility she could not follow, and had to concentrate, to think back to everything which had been said to her of the Blight. It seemed a very distant thing now, so less immediate than it had been when she came down off Bariback Mountain. Part of a former life.

"I don't recall the Blight's bane ever being described," she told him. "Our mages were more concerned with the declaration of war, and did not pursue the matter with our instructor beyond establishing with certainty that it was gone, that it would not threaten Farakkan. The one assigned to teach us the Ibisian language, Kerikath las Dona, said of their attempts to stop it that spells of containment and cancellation had no effect on it, that it was impossible to neutralise. She said that the – that the Kierash went to a mountain called Desana and...drew all the power to himself? A great conjuration, she called it. She did not mention summoning wild magic, did not say what he did with the power to get rid of it. Just spoke of the pyre of his destruction."

A murmur of sound cut short Illukar's response. Medair was close enough to hear the cadences of a wend-whisper, but could not make out the words. The relief in his smile told her enough, and he caught up her hand.

"They have found Tarsus," he said. "Asleep on an island quite five miles from the border. They should be taking him in hand even now."

Medair did not even have time to smile in response. Hard on the heels of Illukar's words came the bloom of power, the sudden and gigantic flare which she had felt only once before. The inevitability she had been dreading. Wild magic.

FIFTEEN

Medair was hurriedly dressing when the next wend-whisper came. The distant roar of wild magic completely overwhelmed her ability to sense such a subtle piece of arcana, but she noticed Illukar wearing that intent, listening-to-nothing expression.

"They have Tarsus," he said, as she joined him at the door. His eyes were full of worry and a kind of angry helplessness. "He woke in shock, and dropped the glass onto stone. It shattered. A foolish accident."

"Did it—?"

"The island is no more. It is the Blight."

He continued out of the room without another word, face frozen in an expressionless mask. Medair realised he was suppressing what passed for fury in an habitually controlled man. The worst had happened, for the stupidest of reasons, and he knew of no way to fix it.

Her own plummeting dismay was complicated something she should say, a thing she should suggest. It seemed impossibly unfair that she was faced with another double-barbed choice – to lose Illukar quickly or slowly – and she was scrabbling frantically for ways to avoid it. Surely they could first try other means of stopping the Blight, try those dispells and nullifications and containments in the hopes of hitting on some combination which all of Sar-Ibis' adepts had failed to find. Or they could send someone else, send Sedesten, Islantar, anyone but Illukar. Craven solutions. If she were mage enough, she would go herself, because it seemed far easier to sacrifice herself for him, than the other way around.

But there wasn't any choice. Nor, she discovered as they descended the main stair, any time for prevarication. Islantar was among those crowded into the entry hall, and his eyes fixed on her with typical determination. He alone would be able to see the same solution to this lost knowledge. Silence wasn't an option for her, if it ever had been.

She was given the briefest of respites, as Illukar swept straight out to the portico at the top of the doubled entrance stairs. The move was some measure of how he was feeling, for there was little to gain by going outside to look in the direction of the raging power. The Blight would not tower into the sky as the Conflagration had. Just dissolve Farakkan quietly into water.

Still, he looked, and she did as well, and saw Falcon Black silhouetted against the sunset above the hills. The half-wrecked castle was grim and ugly and striped incongruously in gold and pink. The Blight was somewhere beyond, an unseen presence shouting its advance.

"Can you call him back?"

When she didn't respond immediately, Islantar went so far as to touch her arm. "I don't know," she said, struggling against her reluctance to call upon the only person who might know how to stop the Blight. She recognised that her hesitation wasn't only due to what it would mean for Illukar, but also because that person was Ieskar.

She didn't want to see Ieskar again, didn't want to try and summon him up, certainly didn't want to ask for his help. In the face of the Blight, that seemed contemptible. But she wasn't certain she knew *how* to summon him, for she hadn't done so consciously, back in Athere. He had simply arrived, possessing Islantar – the nearest of his descendants – and told her things she did not want to hear. And offered to haunt her, if she would not touch his hand.

"Call him back?" Illukar repeated, turning to look from Medair to Islantar. "What do you mean?"

Islantar glanced at the mix of servants and others crowding the doorway, then led Illukar and Medair down to the foot of the twin stair, and the entrance of the lavender-filled garden between them. Only two people followed: Queen Sendel, who wore a most pugnacious expression, and Avahn, slow and unsteady, but awake and on his own feet. Illukar's innate courtesy asserted itself, and Medair was given a few moments more while he saw his injured heir settled on one of the stone seats. It was sufficient time for her to notice, in the shadow of the stair, how that slight glow still clung to Illukar. And to see, like some daemon conjured by thought alone, another tall, luminous figure, wearing clothes so dark that only his face and the straight fall of his unbound hair distinguished him from shadow.

"Funeral clothes," she said inanely, and everyone looked at her, then followed the direction of her gaze.

Kier Ieskar didn't move. He was, as she had said, wearing funeral clothes – the unrelieved black Ibisians reserved for the dead – and his face was thin and drawn. This was how he must have looked when he was placed in his tomb.

When he stepped forward – one of those statue-come-to-life movements which had made him so inhuman to her – she caught a glimpse of stone and leaf directly through him. He was an insubstantial shade from the past, nowhere near as real as he had been when she met him in the crypts, yet every bit as overwhelming as the first time she had laid eyes on him.

"What magic is this?" Queen Sendel asked, and was ignored. Even her vigour was thinned, diminished by the intensity of the dead Kier's presence.

Ieskar's gaze fixed on Illukar's face as he stopped before him. It was a shock to see them together, to mark the similarity of their features and, worse, the duplication in their expressions and their way of holding themselves. Medair clutched at differences. The most apparent was their height, but that observation only made her remember a time, back in Thrence, when she had realised Illukar was not so tall as she expected. A moment of dissonance she now understood: he was shorter than Ieskar.

"My brother," Ieskar said.

"*Ekarrel.*" Illukar bowed, the same degree of courtesy he would award Kier Inelkar, but with an added note of veneration. *Niadril* Kier. She had never asked herself what Illukar would think of the man who had destroyed her peace, had not even allowed herself to consider the question. Far more than a historical figure for both of them.

As Ieskar turned to look at her, Medair forced questions out of her head through sheer effort of will. She knew she must be almost as pale as an Ibisian, but she refused to look as sick as she felt. It was a relief, and something of a shock, when he only inclined his head and moved to study Islantar. Then that pale, piercing gaze returned to Illukar.

"You have little time," Ieskar said, in the most calm and unhurried tone imaginable. "This occurrence is not a precise duplication. By the next sunset, this city will be gone."

"What is it saying?" Queen Sendel asked in Parlance, as both Islantar and Avahn drew in their breath. Illukar did not break the gaze of the ghost who had named him brother.

"Will you tell us how to stop it?" he asked.

Ieskar lifted his hand, a move which would have made Medair flinch if it had been directed at her. Long fingers passed through Illukar's cheek before coming to rest against – or under – his temple. They stood that way ten breaths or more, while their small audience stared and wondered. Medair closed her eyes, because this was Illukar's death sentence and she could only hate Ieskar more for making it possible.

When she looked back, it was as if Ieskar had never been. Queen Sendel had moved to take his place, and was questioning Illukar tersely. Islantar stood at Illukar's shoulder, his composure not equal to hiding tight misery. Avahn had covered his eyes.

It was what Medair could see in Illukar's face which was worst. A certain amount of relief. And resignation.

⚭

Water, reeds, mud, and myriad small islands. Wetter than a swamp, but far too shallow to be a lake. In late twilight, the Shimmerlan was a murky, uncertain expanse of shadows and subdued reflections. It felt threatening and unpleasant and smelled of damp and rot. And everything which could scurry or jump or crawl was running from it.

Insects whirred past Medair's face and birds flew overhead making strange forlorn cries. In the short time since they'd reached the Shimmerlan's border, at least three snakes had slithered by her feet, and there had been frogs and water rats and many things she'd never seen before. All heading away from the oppressive advance of what must look like nothing more than a pool of dark water.

They were waiting for the tracking party, returning ahead of the spreading Blight. With Tarsus, apparently. Medair spent her time watching Illukar's face as he discussed some sort of levitation spell with Sedesten; working out ways for him not to die just long enough to banish the Blight. Medair was taking in little things, like the way Illukar would tip his head ever so slightly to one side when he was considering a request, and the way he held his hands loose and relaxed at his sides, not shifting them about as so many people did.

She couldn't quite believe she was doing this. Cataloguing her lover, snatching at minutiae before he went and saved the world and died. Now should be when she produced another Horn of Farak, another artefact of stupendous power, and this time it wouldn't be too late and she would save what was most important to her and it wouldn't all end in tears.

But artefacts were nothing to wild magic. The Horn of Farak would be little more than a bright firefly against this arcane sun, and all that ridiculously large collection she had brought from Kersym Bleak's hoard were useless dross. All Medair could do was watch, with the rest of the muted crowd who had followed to the Shimmerlan's edge. The sum of her choices now were to make Illukar's departure as hard or easy as possible. To meet loss bravely or to curse it and wail.

That was no choice, either.

"They're coming," said Kel ar Haedrin, though how the woman had seen through the post-twilight gloom Medair couldn't imagine. Still, she was right. A blot of darkness shifted, became distinct figures accompanied by the sound of sloshing boots. And preceded by one of the inhabitants of the Shimmerlan.

Herald N'Taive had called them Alshem. The swimmer-folk. The woman who lifted herself from the water was the size of a ten-year child, though noticeably mature beneath a tightly wrapped leathery sheath. Slender and lithe, with a fine pelt of brown-black covering head, neck, shoulders and arms, she was still far more human than Medair had expected. The eyes were strangest: liquid black, lacking any sign of white, and with a transparent inner lid which slid up instead of down.

The Alshem woman carried herself with an effortless dignity as she approached Illukar, who towered above her looking as distant and remote as only Ibisians can. She made a fluid gesture with her hand and bowed her head to a degree which Medair interpreted as honour without servitude.

"Strange doings, cold one," the Alshem said in precise Ibis-laran. "We have brought the one you required."

"My thanks, sun skimmer," Illukar replied, managing not to sound the least bit uncertain. He'd obviously found a chance to mine Sedesten for information about these neighbours he did not remember. And would only meet once.

Medair looked away, breathing deeply. He was going to die, and she had to sit here and let him. She felt cold and frozen inside, her chest clogged with the effort of not wailing and screaming. So hard not to weep.

"Ibisian."

It was Tarsus' voice, urgent and imperative. He came tramping out of the swamp trailed by the search party. Wet and haggard, the boy looked like the survivor of a shipwreck, his eyes filled with a different kind of agony than that which had consumed him in Falcon Black. There was less anger to it, but a depth Medair recognised.

"He says there's nothing I can do to stop it," Tarsus said, shortly. "Is it true? "

"There is nothing." Illukar's expression was not welcoming.

"Are you *certain*?!" Tarsus mastered desperate anger with evident difficulty. He swallowed a gasping breath, staring at Illukar's face, then straightened. "What then? You have something planned. I can see it in your eyes. What can I do to help?"

Bald anguish, overmastering guilt and a childish horror warred in his voice, all subdued by stern determination. How do you live with the knowledge that the world is dying by an act of yours? That because you could not trust, because you had been taught to hate, to never forgive, you had caused the worst thing possible?

Illukar responded to the patent sincerity of Tarsus' offer. "It is a matter for adepts," he said, more kindly than Medair could have managed. "There is something which might succeed and we go to try it. Farakkan is not yet lost." But that was all the comfort he could give.

Leaving the boy to Kel ar Haedrin, Illukar turned to one of the mud-spattered escort: an angular Farakkian woman in her fifties, who had been shifting uneasily during Tarsus' interlude. "What can you tell me, Kel?"

"It moves at a slow walking pace, Keridahl. Just water on water, though none could mistake the peril. We outpaced it easily, but it will reach this point by midnight."

There was a pause, as everyone took in the urgency of the situation, then it was back to contingency plans and orders. Medair, looking determinedly at nothing, found Islantar again at her elbow and allowed him to draw her a short distance down the sodden bank, till they could barely make out Illukar's glow. The Kierash didn't speak, merely stood beside her, keeping a tight control on his expression as he waited, turning a glowstone over and over in his hands.

When Illukar finally joined them, Islantar stepped forward, lifted a hand, then let it drop. They were both so rarely awkward that the hesitation which followed was painful. Then Islantar collected himself and took another step, so that he was facing Illukar, much as Tarsus had a short while before. The duplication again reminded Medair how very young Islantar was.

"There–" Islantar began, and ground to a halt, staring up at Illukar. Such an Ibisian scene: both their faces were formal masks, their posture correct, pain kept inside where it cut deeper. Yet no-one who looked on them could possibly think Ibisians cold.

"There are so many things I have wished to say to you," Islantar said, his voice just the tiniest fraction higher than normal. "I have looked for an opportunity to tell you that you are – that I have learned so much from you, followed your lead in countless things. You are–"

A father to me. He didn't say it, just looked down, silenced either by his own emotions or by the rules which governed his rank.

Odd that Illukar, considered so perfectly Ibisian, could simply reach out and embrace his Kierash. Islantar's eyes went wide, then he wrapped his arms tightly around Illukar's waist, hiding his face against his chest.

"Make me proud, Islantar," Illukar said into the boy's hair. His face was a mask, but his voice was full of undercurrents. Islantar whispered something so softly Medair was not certain even Illukar could make it out, then let go and stepped back, resuming at least a semblance of his self-command.

"Goodbye," he said simply, then walked away. His steps were steady and his back straight.

Illukar watched him until he was out of sight, then moved toward Medair.

"My turn now?"

He didn't quite smile. "I would that this moment had never come, Medair."

She looked away, out into the roiling dark. The evening was cool, a light breeze toying with her hair, but it was impossible to regard the night as pleasant. It was neither heat nor wind nor visible threat, but the Blight's power was a doom impossible to ignore or mistake. It choked and stifled and crushed, perfectly matching the feelings which welled inside.

Illukar's long fingers curled over her shoulders. "I have requested of Avahn that he care for you. I would like, very much, for you to consider The Avenue your home."

How can it be, when you aren't there? Medair didn't say it, instead turning and clasping his hands. It was hard to look up into his eyes.

"These last few days–" He paused, and she could almost see him think on all that had happened in such a short time. "I know that what we have shared will make my death harder for you, but I cannot regret choosing my moment to speak."

"No." Medair determinedly set aside the selfish, petulant part of herself which regretted ever having met him. And the part which told her that no good could ever have come of lying with a White

Snake. "I'm glad you did," she said, meaning it. "I—" How to say everything she had not? "I have been happy with you," she said, finally, and watched his eyes smile. That made it nearly impossible not to cry, so she followed Islantar's example and hid in Illukar's embrace. So much easier to simply hold him and try to pretend it wasn't for the last time.

Immediately, her memory served up to her the expression on Illukar's face when he had bowed to Ieskar. Such straightforward respect. Did he admire the man who had destroyed her Empire to save his people's pride? Had he been raised on stories of the *Niadril* Kier's war, just as Medarists followed the legend of Medair? What would Illukar have done, in Ieskar's place?

"What is it?" he asked, catching her off guard. He must have read some tension in her body, unless he truly could see into her mind.

"This isn't the moment," she said, aching more with every word. She didn't want to ask him, not now.

"It is the last moment, Medair," he said. Almost wry. "Speak."

Would it be better not to know, and live with the uncertainty? Or should she risk tarnishing her memory of him? She drew back, enough to look up into that faintly glowing face, and saw a shadow of concern. That made it harder to refuse, for she would not leave him wondering as he went off to die.

Her tongue was heavy and reluctant as she spoke. "Kier Ieskar...told me that he invaded because the Ibis-lar would have become a pauper race if they'd accepted the Emperor's mercy. Feared, hated, separated..." She trailed off.

"I have heard the *Niadril* Kier's reasons," Illukar said. His voice had gone quite soft, as if someone held a knife to his heart. Medair stared up at him, a knot in her throat she couldn't swallow.

"Do you think he was right?" she asked, faintly.

"Not for Palladium," Illukar replied, immediately. But his eyes were unhappy. "It was disastrous for the Empire, and so many centuries later there is still division because of it. It is the one great wound in our past that Farakkan cannot forget. As Ibis-lar..." The care with which he weighed his words was answer in itself. "It may not have happened as he forecast. Grevain had offered aid, shelter:

a generous welcome. There was no certainty that they would have devolved into heartless outcasts. I do not doubt they would have been feared for their power, that inevitably they would have been at odds with some Farak-lar, perhaps persecuted. We are not the most flexible people, and the laws which bound us at that time were astoundingly rigid. Being divided, as refugees must be, among those who could house them, they would have been powerfully disadvantaged, overwhelmed by Farakkan's numbers. A vulnerable position." He stopped, then continued grimly. "In the longest of terms, yes. It was not an honourable thing to do, but for the Ibis-lar as a people, I think he was right."

There were so many implications to this admission that Medair's head spun. And yet, it barely mattered.

"Strange how little difference that makes to the way I'm feeling now," she said in astonishment, and kissed him because it was true.

Too soon someone – Sedesten – came near them and said: "It is ready." When Illukar drew back she had to force herself not to cling to him, and instead tried one last time to conjure some plan for his survival out of need and nothing. All she could manage was a wretched attempt at hiding the way her breath sobbed in her throat.

"I will miss you, always," she said. His attempt at a smile was sadly awry, out of place on Illukar's beautifully drawn features. It was her pain, her loss, which was doing that to him.

"I will love you always, Medair," he said, a stark statement which did not pretend that his 'always' would not be longer than that night. He brushed her cheek once with those slender white fingers, then turned and walked away.

Hidden by the dark, Medair curled down to hug her knees, closed her teeth on the hand pressed to her mouth, and howled.

SIXTEEN

It was the longest stretch of nothing she'd ever known.

Illukar had been planning to travel near to the centre of the Blight, to try to avoid destroying Finrathlar's western hills, but Medair had no idea how long the journey would take. Such drawn-out tenterhooks had left her with a conflicting desire for it to be over, and for it to never happen. Sitting forever in the dark, on chill, marshy earth, would be a small price to pay for Illukar's life, wouldn't it? But she supposed that would mean he would be eternally traveling to his death, and she wouldn't have that, either.

The Blight was getting close. Drained and weary, she stared out into the night. Few birds flew past now, but the supply of insects seemed never-ending. Medair pictured all Farakkan's inhabitants, every species, crowding to the edges of an ever-expanding lake, then discarded the thought. Hardly a happy thing to picture Illukar's sacrifice as futile.

"Keris an Rynstar."

She watched dispassionately as Islantar approached, carrying a glowstone. "I'm not going to hurl myself in, if that's what brings you."

"No. You would not do that to him."

Islantar sounded more certain of that than Medair was herself. She didn't bother to gainsay him, watching him arrange himself into an attitude of polite attention. Court posture. This was more than solicitude, then.

"There is one who wishes to speak to you," he said.

"I have no wish for company, Kierash."

"I am aware of that. I ask this of you, Keris."

Again that was the kind of request Emperor Grevain had been wont to make: refusal was not easy. Medair looked up into

Islantar's young, resolute face and sighed silently. "Very well," she said, standing. Islantar waited a moment, then gestured with the glowstone.

Two figures approached along the bank, gradually resolving into dark-haired, copper-complected young men of similar build. There was, Medair noticed, a similarity in their features which suggested blood ties. Tarsus and Thessan. She supposed it was not improbable that Xarus Estarion might have decided to join his own line with the Corminevars, but these brotherly countenances were the first suggestion she'd encountered of such a union. What, she wondered, had happened to Tarsus' mother? And what were the implications for the succession of the Decian throne?

Those questions, however, were not why these two had come to see her. Prince Thessan looked like he'd rather be anywhere else. Tarsus, only marginally less ragged than her previous sighting of him, was evidently the one who wanted to speak to her. Behind the two young men emerged a half-dozen guards, headed by Kel ar Haedrin. They remained just at the edge of the circle of light cast by Islantar's glowstone, none of them completely hiding their concern.

Tarsus sketched a gesture of courtesy. He seemed to be as high in formal ropes as Islantar. Thessan just looked sour.

"Herald an Rynstar–" Tarsus began, and Medair shook her head.

"I lost my role as Herald, Lord Tarsus." The title she gave him sat awkwardly on her tongue, but it would take too long to decide the correct formal way to address someone who might be the true descendent of an ousted Emperor. She would rather they just went away.

"Forfeited it, you mean," put in Thessan, at no pains to hide the anger and disdain in his voice. "When you sided with White Snakes over Palladians."

Medair shook her head, ignoring the sick knot which had instantly formed in her stomach. "It was not a matter of choice, Prince Thessan. I stopped being a Herald of the Empire when I woke five hundred years after the Palladian Empire's fall."

"How convenient for you," Thessan snapped. "With your oath magically dissolved, you're free to take up with whatever White Snake catches your eye."

"Leave to, Thes," Tarsus said, putting a restraining hand on Thessan's arm. He appeared torn between agreeing with the Prince and the knowledge that Illukar – a White Snake – was giving his life to stop a disaster Tarsus had sparked. "Lady an Rynstar, then," he said. "I wished to ask you of Emperor Grevain. You knew him–"

"I was sworn to him," Medair said, softly.

"Yes. You served him." Tarsus brushed at his curly hair, as if looking for a delay. "It has been put to me that...to press my claim to the Silver Throne is not in Palladium's best interests. I would know–"

"You would let yourself be talked out of what is yours by right!" Thessan said hotly, subsiding only when Tarsus gave him a pained, pleading look. It was obvious that there was considerable affection between the pair. And that Thessan would happily throw Medair and Islantar into the Blight, if not for the guards who watched.

"Let me do this, Thes," Tarsus muttered, then met Medair's eyes squarely. "I would know what Emperor Grevain would do, at such a pass. Whether he would approve of my quest."

"I can't answer for the Emperor," Medair said, dismayed. "Nor," she added, glancing at Thessan's angry face, "would you have any way of knowing if I was honest in any opinion I gave you."

"I am aware of that, Lady an Rynstar," said Tarsus. "But you alone of all the world have met the Emperor. You witnessed the invasion, you quested to stop it, no matter what the outcome. Truth or lie, I feel I need to hear what you have to say. What kind of man was he? Would he have surrendered his crown to benefit his people?"

Medair blinked, trying to bend her mind away from her grief, to think along unfamiliar courses. The intensity of power emitted by the Blight made it impossible to forget that Illukar was out there, preparing to die because of this boy. Grevain Corminevar seemed so impossibly long ago.

"I...cannot really picture him as anything but Emperor," she said, slowly. "He was born to the rule. If he had survived Athere's fall, if he had been – if he had been allowed to live after Kier Ieskar took the Silver Throne..." She shook her head blankly. "No, the situations are too dissimilar. If the Emperor, instead, had woken as I did, five hundred years too late, would he have raised an army to take back his throne?" She thought about the ever-busy, abrupt man she had sworn her life to, and realised how little she knew of him. To her, he was Lord and Law and there was no bond of friendship. Simply Emperor, the ruler she had so admired.

"This is useless," Thessan muttered, and Medair searched her memory, not willing to leave Tarsus completely unanswered.

"He was a proud man," she said, carefully. "Wise to the political games. He offered his opinions rarely, for his every word was weighted. He disliked intensely things not going to order. He would give second chances, but never a third." She remembered Grevain's manner when he sat in judgment over some dispute. It gave her more confidence. "If he had found himself in today's Palladium, he might well have sought his throne," she said, looking directly into Tarsus' eyes. "If he believed that it would benefit Palladium, if he thought Ibisian rule, in practice, was unjust. But I don't believe he would feel that way."

"That's just what *you* would say," Thessan snapped, predictably. "But Ibisian rule is anything *but* just. How many true Palladians do you see in power? How many rise from beneath the White Snake boot?"

Medair stared at him, realising that Thessan knew less of the reality of Palladium than she did, no matter what changes the Conflagration had made. How could she tell him that very few Palladians seemed to object to Ibisians? That those who still nurtured hatreds were a minority, no matter how powerful their effect on their land. It was obvious that, whether it had been greed or justice which motivated Xarus Estarion, Thessan truly did believe Decia's war had been to benefit Palladians.

"I won't pretend that most of those who rule aren't of Ibisian descent," she said, trying to be absolutely fair. "That is hardly surprising, when titles are hereditary. And Ibisians are not thought arrogant merely by accident. But I have seen no suffering. Or any indication that laws are interpreted in the favour of Ibis-lar over Farak-lar. Though hampered by Medarists and perhaps the pure camp of Ibisians, Palladians as a whole are prospering. It is only my opinion, but I do not think Emperor Grevain would overset that, simply to replace Kier Inelkar on the Silver Throne.

Tarsus' reaction was overwhelmed by Thessan's. "You could hardly give us any other answer," he said, in a low, trembling voice. "I will not forget what you have done. You killed those who would have redressed the old wrong–"

"No." Medair said the word flatly, angrily. "I defended Athere against an invasion. Stop trying to fight a five-hundred year past war."

Tarsus again restrained his fellow, gripping Thessan's arm tightly, then asked in a quieter, but no less accusative tone: "Can you deny that there are those in Palladium who wish to be freed from White Snake tyranny?"

Medair had to force herself not to simply send them away so she could return to mourning. Or give in to the very large part of her which wanted to slap Tarsus, to shriek and tear his hair and ask him how he dared to show himself before her when he had ignored their warnings, when he had run with that mirror, and let it fall and brought Illukar's death down on him and left her with no way out.

She took a breath, slow and deep.

"Of course I can't. What you refuse to let yourself acknowledge is that they are not the only 'true' Palladians." Medair gestured past Tarsus, to the row of guards silently watching them, and flame-haired Liak ar Haedrin with her Ibisian uniform and creamy skin. "Were you going to liberate her from Ibisian rule? Or kill her along with the White Snakes you hate so much?"

Tarsus looked at Kel ar Haedrin for a long moment, and the Velvet Sword blinked back impassively. "The White Snake invasion was wrong," he said, apparently trying to rebuild the foundations of his animosity.

"Yes. And the Empire defended itself."

"They *stole* the throne!"

"They conquered Palladium," Medair said. "Five hundred years ago. And became part of it."

"What of those who don't think White Snakes are a part of Palladium? What of those who raise their voices to me, to the true heir of that line, and ask for their freedom? Should I just ignore them?"

"Perhaps not." Medair looked at him, and her own anger faded. So earnest, so impassioned. But no longer sure that hate was the way. "Where would the killing have stopped, Tarsus? How many would it have taken, before you considered Palladium cleansed? Would you have killed all who were pale, or over-tall, just to be sure? Or would it be permitted to have a quarter Ibisian blood? An eighth? People who have lived in Palladium all their lives, who think of themselves as Palladian, who speak Parlance and who would consider you the invader? Will you also oust those who are Farakkian blood who have been appointed by Ibisians? Yes, you could make the Ibisians pay, but is it worth destroying Palladium in the process?"

"It can't be forgotten," Thessan broke in. "It can't just be put aside. They will always be invaders, they will always have been the ones who made war. They can't be allowed to live." His voice was a pitch higher than usual, and he said the words as if he repeated a child's well-worn lesson, a litany to block out any doubt. "A war does not finish merely because the victors have claimed the prize."

"What is your position, then, Thessan, by that way of thinking? Decia just invaded. Should that never be forgiven? Should Palladians not tolerate Decians to live?"

"No doubt the White Snakes are greedy for our land–" Thessan retorted, hotly, but Islantar's cool voice slid into the fray.

"Palladium has no interest in expanding her borders," the Kierash said, with serene confidence. Thessan rounded on him as if looking for relief in action, and Medair saw the guards surge forward a step. Islantar didn't move.

Held back, perhaps by the utter calm in the Kierash's eyes, Thessan did no more than clench his fists. "The White Snakes are the problem," he said, desperately stubborn. "Without the White

Snakes, there would be no war. Farakkan would be united once again."

Medair sighed softly. "I doubt it," she said. It was as much an admission to herself as anything. "The Ibisians invaded, true, but the Empire fell because the West took the opportunity it had been given."

Tarsus lifted a hand as if pushing that argument away. "The West was used by the White Snakes," he said, tightly.

"The West broke free of a conqueror. Don't you see? Clinging to old grievances raises older ghosts. The West longed to go back to its old, fractured, fractious ways, but the Empire was too strong until the invasion. A Corminevar conquered Decia once. Made it a part of the Empire and installed a Duke. If you look back far enough, there was a time when Athere's hill overlooked the grazing land of some cow-lord who had never heard of Corminevars."

Thessan shook his head, as if he had a bee trying to beat its way out of his skull. "This leads us nowhere. Cow-lords, the old disputes with the West. We are talking about *now*."

"Yes. We are." It was Tarsus who said it, holding his head very high and still. "Thank you, Lady an Rynstar. I will – I am obliged for your opinion." He took Thessan's arm in a tight grip and, with obvious effort, turned and walked through the line of guards and into the night.

"He's thinking about it," Medair said when she and Islantar were alone. Half Kel ar Haedrin's contingent remained, but had withdrawn so that they were barely visible. "Though perhaps bringing Thessan along was a mistake. He obviously has influence over Tarsus."

"But it is Prince Thessan I must convince," Islantar reminded her. "Tarsus might be used as he has been already, but unless we remove Queen Sendel's line from Decia's throne, Prince Thessan is the one who will fund a cause which should be long dead. And he does not have Tarsus' depth of empathy, nor the shock of causing this." Islantar glanced toward the Blight, and his face tightened. It could not be long, now, before Illukar attempted to stop what Tarsus had begun.

"I have asked Queen Sendel to allow me them both, for a year's visit in Athere," Islantar continued. "And in that time–" He looked into the dark in the direction the Decian pair had gone. "Tarsus is already beginning to see that a ruler is owned by the people, not the other way around. Perhaps his ties to Thessan will be strong enough to bend the more rigid of that pair. And with both of them, and you, I may be able to weaken this eternal clutching of an old grievance to each new generation's breast. The deaths of the past days will be a vivid wound, of course, but I can hope to ease it once the hurdle of the old is overcome."

"Were you ever given the chance to be a child, Kierash?" Medair asked, feebly. Islantar looked surprised, then smiled.

"For a short while. Even in my family, there is a childhood. But no more escape from the burdens of position than Tarsus." He paused, and then added with stark honesty, "Not killing him is the hardest thing I have ever done."

Medair felt a tremor run through her, and bit down on her lip, nodding, and so glad of him in that moment, sharing her loss.

He was holding himself very straight, eyes wide, and held out his hand. "I give you my name, Keris. I would ask that I might use yours."

"Of course," Medair said, automatically gripping the slim, pale fingers.

"Thank you, Medair." That young-old face briefly relaxed, then firmed, Kierash once more. "I have a more difficult request."

"You want me to help with the hurdle."

"Yes." He nodded, his glance a mix of gratitude and concern. "I know it is not a role you are eager to assume, but you saw the power of your words on Tarsus. It is not merely that you are Medair an Rynstar, long made legend, but that you were *there*. And that for you, the war is over. I ask that you allow me to use that."

Medair looked away from him. She wanted little more than to find herself another Bariback, run away from all which could remind her of Illukar, and weep. But she wouldn't. She thought, hoped, that she had reached beyond such cowardice.

"I used the Horn," she pointed out. "All the fury, grief and outrage which is the consequence of that will focus on me. You may find I cause more damage than good."

"Even hating you, they will want to hear. You said it yourself: at least they will know your reasons."

It would be a life of being spat at. Not a weapon to save an Empire, not a path of honour and glory, but a fumbling kind of recompense which would do nothing to dull the loss of Illukar. How could she stand it?

"I will try," she told Islantar, and saw him stand straighter. Relieved. He had not been certain of her.

"I am glad of that," he said, then looked down. The power of the Blight thrummed all around them. "Will you come back to The Avenue now?" he asked, and his voice had lost some of its strength.

"I would rather stay here."

Islantar looked at her intently, then nodded. "I will return for you in the morning."

He started to turn away but she reached out and again caught one of his hands. "I think the Emperor would find you worthy of his throne," she said, thickly. "And I think you will make him proud." It was not Grevain she meant. "Good luck."

"I shall make my own luck," Islantar replied, the light from the glowstone shimmering in his eyes. "It seems the safer course."

He returned the pressure of her hands briefly, and followed Tarsus and Thessan into the night. Medair watched him go, then turned to find Kier Ieskar at her side.

SEVENTEEN

edair did not flinch or cry out. Too much had happened for her to even be startled. She clenched her jaw and took a deep breath, but was able to stand quietly while Ieskar looked in Islantar's direction. He was as he had appeared in the garden of The Avenue: transparent and luminescent, clad for death. When the glow of Islantar's stone had been swallowed by the night, Ieskar turned on Medair the unfeeling gaze she had long thought to hate. He was drawn and wasted, the fine bones of his face standing out clearly beneath his pale skin, but the cold expressionless mask was the same.

"Did I summon you this time," she asked, unsteadily, "or is this excursion on your own account?"

"A little of both, perhaps." His soft, composed voice was exactly as she remembered it. "I wish to mark my brother's passing. You would like very much for me to find a way for Illukar to live."

"And will you?"

"I cannot." There was a ghost of honest regret in the words, and the knot of hope which had clutched Medair's chest unravelled. She turned away to look out at the night, wishing for miracles. None came, of course. The Blight still beat invisibly at her across the ever-decreasing Shimmerlan. Ieskar didn't suddenly produce a solution, or even go away and leave her alone. She felt poorly served.

"He's not your brother," she said abruptly, unable to stand his silent presence at her back.

"Merely a descendent of his line?" Ieskar was unperturbed by her denial. "You are wrong. Illukar does not remember the past, but that does not make him any less my brother."

She looked over her shoulder at him, but that was pointless. There was never any expression on Ieskar's face. "He was reborn to face the Blight?" The idea sickened her.

"Perhaps." Ieskar gazed out over the water. "It is the fourth time he has lived, only to have that life cut short. As if the first sacrifice was imprinted onto the world itself."

"Born to die."

Ieskar did not deny it. "The cycle may be broken this time. He has no children, and it is unlikely that he would be reborn outside the direct path of descent."

"Is that meant to be comforting?"

"No." Ieskar's cold blue gaze did not waver from the dark water, but he moved one of his hands, a gesture she could not interpret. "Illukar faced the Blight because I did not," he added. "It was my place to do so."

"What? Then why–?"

"Sar-Ibis was dying," he said, as if that would explain it. When she only stared, he went on. "The Ibis-lar ensured the health of the land by binding it to the Kier. As Sar-Ibis failed, so did I, until I did not have strength enough to face the Blight, though it was my role. Eventually I had not strength enough to live." There was still no flicker of expression on his face. "It is possible that the substitution is the reason why I endure and Illukar dies and dies again."

"Why you *endure*?" Medair repeated, feeling ever less capable of dealing with this encounter. "You are not–?"

He looked at her then, shifting first his gaze then turning so he faced her. Tall and upright and eternally composed. "I am not a construct of Estarion's Conflagration."

It was something which she had not properly thought about, but which had lurked at the back of her thoughts. She'd half-believed this ghost Ieskar to be conjured from her own memories, given form by wild magic. But then, like Finrathlar, he would not even know the truth of his own existence.

"My memories are those of the past known to you," Ieskar said, reading either her thoughts or the expression on her face. She stood staring at him, at the trailing sleeves of his funeral robe and the way his pale hair was untouched by the wind, and that unwavering gaze which had haunted her longer than he'd been dead. And she had to turn away.

"Will Islantar succeed?" she asked, to stop herself from thinking of either Illukar or Ieskar. She felt like she'd been running. Ieskar didn't oblige her with an answer, so she covered her unease by finding herself another rock to sit on, too aware of his steady gaze.

"He appears determined to try," Ieskar said, after an interminable pause. "There are routes other than conciliation."

This provided her with a revivifying spurt of anger. "Should those who can't forgive the invasion be driven out, then? Or simply be suppressed, ignored? You would watch Tarsus relinquish his claim to the throne, but have nothing given back? Shouldn't Islantar make some meaningful sacrifice?"

The mask gave her nothing. "You are adept at both sides of this argument, Keris."

"I have seen both sides," she said, hotly. "I don't see a solution."

"It is possible that there is no solution," Ieskar replied, serenely. "Not for every side, every interest. Islantar will try to find some balance, a way of easing the hatreds. I think it likely that he will be more inclined to listen to matters of redress than many of his predecessors. As for sacrifices—" He turned again to look out over the Shimmerlan. "He has already begun to pay."

Medair felt as if she had been punched in the stomach. She drew in an unsteady breath and tried not to lose herself. Her anger was gone as if it had never been and she felt only helpless hurt. For a bare moment anger had taken her thoughts from Illukar, from that fact that he was going to die, that there was no way to save him.

There was.

The odd certainty which had preyed on her at Falcon Black returned. There was something which could be done. She knew it like she had known that Vorclase had been waiting. But how? Had Ieskar told her the truth, when he'd said there was nothing he could do to save Illukar? She'd never known the Ibisian Kier to lie, but Medair was certain she would not be able to read him one way or the other: Illukar was transparent by comparison. If there was something Ieskar knew, how could she winkle it out of him?

The idea of trying to manipulate the Kier was ludicrous. She looked at his luminescent figure out of the corner of her eye and decided that she would not attempt it. But she would ask.

"Did you tell me the full truth," she began, hesitantly, "when you said there was no way to stop Illukar's death? Is there, perhaps, something I could do? Someone who is – who is not dead?"

Ieskar turned his head minutely. "Did you tell me the full truth, when I asked why you hunted the Horn?"

Medair tried to say something. Her mouth worked, but nothing came out. What could she say? Could she *not* answer, when Illukar's life was in the balance? But Ieskar was not bargaining for a response.

"Yes, there is something which could be done," he said, evenly. "As I am, I cannot cast. I have no reservoir of power, no means of impacting the world about me. But I could possess one of my blood, even one of limited strength, and be able to face the Blight. Whom do you suggest?"

Medair immediately thought of Islantar, and was forced to shake her head. "Illukar wouldn't accept that," she said, unhappily.

"No." He didn't say any more, simply watched her. Waiting for an answer to the question he had asked.

"It was true," she said, faint protest to a demand she wished she was only imagining. "I decided to hunt for the Horn after your brother's child came to you."

Ieskar still didn't respond, just stood there, eyes cutting through her as if she held the gate device to her chest. How she hated this man. The man who, if he had not been leading an invasion – but even then all the laws which constrained a Kier–

Medair wrenched her mind away. It wasn't so. The similarities to Illukar meant nothing: they were different at core. Ieskar had never smiled, not once; he lacked one of the things she treasured most about Illukar.

And, whispered a traitorous voice at the back of her mind, what reason did Ieskar have to smile? His home had been destroyed. He was leading an invasion against overwhelming odds. He was dying. And you hated him.

Taking a shaky, shallow breath, Medair stared into pale blue eyes. "When you carried Kierash Adestan away...the light reflected from your cheek."

She thought she'd never seen a face more utterly closed. "You left because I wept." So soft she was unsure she'd heard the words correctly.

"I left because I wanted to stop you."

"I understand."

There was absolution in the words; exactly what Medair didn't want to hear. She lashed out rather than accept. "Why is there nothing you can do? If he died in your place before, why can't you find a way to stop it from happening again? Why are you here with me instead of saving him?!" Medair couldn't look to see the expression on his face and lifted a hand, fingers splayed, to hide her tears. She didn't know if she was crying because Illukar was going to die, or because Ieskar already had.

⁂

When she could finally bring herself to look up again, Ieskar was gone. Perhaps she had managed to wish him away. Or had he been released somehow by her admission that it had been the sight of his tears which sent her questing for the Horn? Because it was the foundation of a harder truth: if he hadn't been on the wrong side of a war she would have more than admired him.

Now there was no war. Ieskar was dead. And Illukar was about to die. Even on Bariback Mountain, she'd never felt this alone.

At that moment, the 'sound' of the Blight faltered. Out in the dark, a white spark was struck to life, and Medair gasped: a pointless intake of breath which did little more than show how stupidly she'd clung to hope. Illukar had begun his counterspell, and all Medair could do was dig her fingernails into the palms of her hands and watch.

What kind of life would she have had anyway, married to Illukar? Hated by two extremes for allying herself with the Ibisians. The Medarists would never forgive her for turning her back on the legend they had built up around her name. The Ibisian purists would do all they could to ensure the Cor-Ibis line remained unsullied. And all the people in between could not help but regard her as a curiosity, a political hot potato. Marriage to Illukar would have inevitably meant that even those protecting her would have reason to kill her.

Medair smiled painfully at the point of light in the far distance. She was not succeeding in convincing herself that she was better off.

The force of the Blight seemed to inhale, growing more intense and more distant at the same time. Medair refused to close her eyes or look away as a white sun flared into being, bringing with it a peculiarly flat dawn. He was too far away for her to see more than the light and the narrow band of reeds and muddy tussocks which separated her from an unbroken stretch of water reaching to the blaze on the horizon.

The pyre of his destruction.

EIGHTEEN

Mist began to lift off the water as the sky paled toward dawn. Medair watched the world expand in the growing light while contracting behind walls of white tendrils. During the long stretch between midnight and dawn, her grief had lost that first torn metal edge, had turned to a numb loss which seemed to clamp her in place. This amorphous white world was well-suited to her apathetic state.

A distant peeping teased at the edge of her hearing as the mist thickened. It was a call she didn't recognise, a chirping sound which seemed to be moving toward her from the left. Occasionally she could make out an accompanying splash, but the source didn't break into view until it was almost in front of her. A flat boat poled by a diminutive figure was drifting through the band of shallow, reed-studded water near the bank.

It was one of the Alshem: a slight, delicate man with a crest of pale hair, his attention focused on dark shapes in the water around the boat. Medair blinked slowly, realising these were otters. They called to each other; disappearing under the black water, returning to the boat, then launching themselves out again. Fine ropes were attached to miniature harnesses about their chests, and a heavy burden of silver dangled from their mouths as they clambered over the low wooden sides. Fish.

Indifferent to sacrifice and near-disaster, the Alshem was collecting the fish brought to the boat, filling his baskets with them. The catch seemed plentiful, and Medair supposed that the fish which fled from the Blight had not moved out into the great, empty stretch of water which it had left behind.

Resenting this illustration of life going on without Illukar, Medair turned her face away and saw...Illukar.

He had lost shoes and demi-robe from his orderly ensemble, was clad only in near-transparent white shirt and breeches as he walked slowly along the bank toward her. His head was bowed, and his hair streamed over his shoulders and down his back, slick with water. He glowed, brighter than ever.

Each step he took had that precise care she recalled from his recuperation from spell-shock, and everything about him looked drained and worn. Even the scratch on his cheek was blanched and puckered. How long had he been in the water?

Medair didn't so much jump up as was jerked to her feet by disbelief. And then she ran, hurled herself on him, dizzily landing kisses on his chin and cheek before wrapping her arms tightly about his waist. He flinched, which gave her a moment of horror until she remembered the deep bruises on his back and hastily readjusted her hold. His response was slow, as if weary determination had frozen him beyond anything other than walking, but then his arms wrapped around her as tightly as she could want.

"How?" she asked, imprinting her cheek with the buttons of his shirt. She could not believe the world had turned upside down so completely. "How?"

Illukar stood very still, one hand cupping the nape of her neck, the other at her waist, fingers digging into her ribs. "Medair..." he said softly, breath stirring strands of hair on the crown of her head. The tone was all wrong. Not relieved or joyous or even simply weary, but full of loss and regret. Medair pulled away enough to look up at his face, and then her throat turned to treacle and ice and her stomach fell into cavernous dismay. Because his eyes were blue.

⌘

Wrenching backwards, Medair stumbled on a tussock of grass and fell inelegantly to the ground. Illukar's eyes shifted from blue to grey, then to a darker blue-grey as he stood looking at her, sprawled at his feet. Then he sighed and sat down on the rock which had been her seat during her interminable night. His eyes shifted back to grey, then blue again.

"Your eyes keep changing colour," Medair told him, clutching at the ground as it spun beneath her.

Obligingly his eyes shifted to blue-grey as he held out his hands, palm down, studying them. Slender, tapering fingers and neatly trimmed nails. The right hand was a different shape from the left: narrower, and a touch longer. And there was a thin scar across the back of the fingers.

"H-how?" Medair said again, as her insides continued to tumble into some bottomless well. She had fallen into a pit of disbelief and there was no escaping it.

His eyes were grey now. Illukar's eyes, full of that dreadful, hateful regret. "Kier Ieskar tried to die in my place," he said, voice even softer than usual. "By taking flesh through me, shielding me and making himself the focus of what I was casting. But the spell was by far too powerful for such subtleties." His eyes flicked to blue-grey as he lifted his hands, then grey as he added: "This is the result."

This. His eyes. That hand. The face, almost the same, but with a change to his mouth which made it far more Ieskar's than Illukar's. And perhaps there was a shade of difference in the line of his jaw. She couldn't decide whether he was taller. It really didn't matter.

Trying to collect herself, Medair shifted to a sitting position, not ready to risk her feet. "You are both – this is both of you?" she asked, hardly able to say it but needing to know precisely what she was dealing with. A few moments ago, she would have done anything to have him back. But Ieskar? "What – how, exactly, both?"

His eyes had been blue again, watching her, but shifted to grey as he spoke. "I doubt there is a way to wholly articulate it. During the casting, I was aware of...Ieskar, but only as a separate presence. I had little concentration to spare." He glanced at the water behind her, the empty stretch beyond the reeds eloquent commentary on the magnitude of the force he had quenched. "At one point I am certain we were physically two, for though it was my reserves being drained, I was no longer the focus. But the spell – the entire purpose of the spell is to concentrate the power to one point and at the zenith–" Illukar turned, as if trying to look at someone beside him. "The focus tried to shift back to me, then it split and it seemed all would end in failure. Then–"

He shook his head, eyes blue, blue-grey, grey. "Then I was in water and there was no power at all. My reserves were empty and I was–" He paused, evidently searching for words, and she again watched the colours cycle. "It is as if – when a healer examines you after an illness, and taps your knee to see your response. Your leg moves, though you did not will it, yet it is still your leg, and it was part of you which moved it." He lifted his right hand and studied it thoughtfully, eyes still grey. "In the first few moments I came close to drowning, because I would move, try to stop myself from moving, try to move. We both very quickly had to learn how to be a passenger, to...take turns, so to speak."

He turned his hand over, equivocally, then looked back at Medair. She tried to summon some sort of meaningful response, but first had to take a deep breath and let it out. It seemed important not to let her voice wobble.

"You...he is trapped in you? Can he be...freed?"

"I am as much trapped in him as he is in me," Illukar replied, flicking a glance back at his hands. "At times, I can hear his thoughts. Sometimes there is nothing to distinguish between what is Ieskar and what is Illukar." His eyes shifted to blue and it was Ieskar who met her gaze directly and, not trying to soften the blow, said: "There is no going back."

How do you reconcile two things which shouldn't exist together? She truly did hate Ieskar. Impossible for her not to. He had invaded Palladium, he had been the aggressor, the one in the wrong and it was no lie or prevarication when she had said she despised him for it. That was true.

The problem, the reason she had run, had been because he was not hateful *enough*. His war had, by his terms, been necessary, and he had prosecuted it according to the rules of his people. An enemy should be wrong, should be detestable and greedy and loathsome, but Ieskar, though alien, had waged his war honourably, had minimized deaths, had acted out of what even she had to admit was a belief that it was necessary for the Ibis-lar. And he had held his brother's child in his arms and shown that he could weep.

She had been attracted all along, in a way. But watching him comfort Adestan had made Medair all too aware of her desire: to touch the untouchable, to comfort him in turn. She had glimpsed something in herself, and she had hated her response to him so much that her reaction had been to seek out the Horn of Farak in the hopes of destroying his entire race.

Five hundred years could not help but alter things, but it did not change the fact of Ieskar's invasion. He had made that choice. The war was over, and he had shown them how to stop the Blight, and saved Illukar, but that did not make him any less Ieskar. The White Snake she hated most. The one she could never forgive.

ℬ

They were just sitting there now, silent. Illukar, only a few feet away, was as distant as the sun, because he was Ieskar. She couldn't remove one from the other, any more than she could separate true Palladians from Ibisian invaders. Hating Ieskar would mean turning her back on Illukar, because would not be possible for her to ignore the fact that he was simply Ieskar 'cleaned up', because he now *was* Ieskar. Every word, every touch she shared with Illukar, she would be sharing with Ieskar, and she hated him, so she could not stay with Illukar. It was impossible to have one without the other.

She had run from her feelings for Ieskar, she had run from the disaster of her belated return, and the schemes of the Decians to include her in war. Could she run from Illukar?

But how to do anything else?

Could she do what Islantar was trying to do with those who tore at Palladium from within? What Ileaha had said she would do with Avahn? Could she forgive Ieskar for being on the wrong side? Can anyone just choose to forgive?

For all she had said to Tarsus, Medair did not see how she could simply stop hating. She had not known if Ileaha would succeed in trying to forgive Avahn for something as innocent as not seeing what was under his nose. She was not certain it was in any way possible for her to make that angry hating part of herself simply close the book on the invasion. The part of herself that said Ieskar should pay for his crimes, no matter the cost.

"Medair." His eyes were grey, watching her face, but she could not read what they held. "I do not hold you to the understanding we had," Illukar said, carefully. "I know very well the consequences of this."

Making an indistinct gesture at himself, he rose to his feet, looking very much as if he was only just able to keep himself upright. "Islantar was to leave a small detachment on guard near the foothills."

He began to walk, summoning fragile poise with such effect that she was reminded of the time he had shown her around Pelamath. Even wet, exhausted and bedraggled, Illukar could be beautiful. And his shield of Ibisian courtesy could not begin to hide the effort it cost him to walk away.

He was trying to make it easy for her. Such unbearable grace. She had to blink hard to stop tears when she saw through the web of his unbound hair and his thin, wet shirt the mottled pattern of the bruises he'd earned during their arrival at Finrathlar. It was like seeing straight through to the pain beneath that determinedly upright carriage.

"Wait," she said, catching up, not quite able to touch him. He paused and she faced him, feeling like the world was not really there as she said through a strangling throat: "I'm not willing to simply give up."

His face was a mask as his eyes flickered from blue-grey to grey, to icy blue. It was Ieskar who lifted his hand, his right hand with that thin scratch across the back of the fingers, until it brushed her stomach. Medair took a deep, fluttery breath as he settled his hand against her ribs, below her left breast. Her heart was racing as if she had run all the way to Athere, and she had to struggle to hold that icy gaze. And he just stood there while her body betrayed her feelings.

"You have hated me for years," he said, in the most obviously controlled voice she'd ever heard from him.

She felt tears sting, because it was true. Her own argument. She refused to give in to it, to the part of her which could not believe what she was doing. "I hated you for a reason that no longer exists."

His only reaction was the tiniest drop of his eyelids. "I will always be the one who ordered Palladium's invasion."

"And the one who made it possible to save Farakkan. And Illukar. Yes, I hated you. And wanted – wanted more of you. Those two things couldn't exist together, so I gave into one and ran from the other. I thought I would kill every single Ibisian in Farakkan, given the chance."

She felt her face heat and took a deep breath. "I don't have the right reasons to hate you, any more. Habit is not enough."

The hand on her ribs shifted, sending shivers all through her chest and stomach. She straightened, an involuntary reaction not entirely negative, and his hand dropped. The blue eyes flickered to grey, then blue again, but not a muscle shifted. Ieskar gave so little away.

"Medair." He said the name with the conscious awareness that she'd never given it to him to use. He even took a breath before going on, a near-hesitation she'd never seen before. "You cannot even bear my touch. How can you think to marry me? Hold me each night in your arms? Bear my children? Can you truly tell me, you with your heart leaping over itself in fright, that you can be my lover? My friend and helpmeet, my comfort and passion? Because I would not accept less."

His eyes were frightening and she realised it was because he held them so fully and absolutely on her, never wavering. She had every scrap of his attention.

"I'm telling you that I want to try," she said, in the faintest of voices, and his eyes flicked suddenly to grey. Illukar, frowning, took both her hands and led her to a pair of rocks. He was fighting exhaustion to have this conversation, and as they sat down it showed as clear as morning.

Before letting go of her hands, he squeezed them tightly, then asked: "Are you saying this for my sake?"

Her throat tightened, but she thrust back the wholly inappropriate sense of insult. There was still a little of the proud herald in her it seemed. "I have never spoken more truth in my life," she said, steadily. "I mightn't be able to simply choose to forgive, but I can work at it. And I am going to. For you, yes, but also because–" She looked down, then back at him and watched as they shifted back to blue. "For my sake, don't you see? I have loved you for as long as I've hated you, Ieskar. I wanted you and I could not stop, though I tried. Now – it's long past time for me to acknowledge that you did what was best for your people instead of mine. And let myself do what's best for me. I don't want to lose either of you."

He just looked at her, the statue Kier she knew so well, trying to stare into her mind as if for the first time he was uncertain what he would find there. His eyes changed back to Illukar's grey, but he did not speak.

"What do you think we should do, Illukar?" she asked.

Those grey eyes lit with the elusive amusement she found so special. "Medair, there is no force in this world which could urge me to argue you out of sharing my bed. If you truly feel yourself capable of it, I think we should go home."

The smile she should have given him in response went all awry and she pressed the base of her palms into her eyes to try and stop them from stinging. "I very much want to hold you to the understanding we had."

But Illukar's face had become Ieskar's blue-eyed mask, shadowed and unyielding.

"You don't believe me," she said. "Do you?"

He didn't reply straight away, examining her expression in minute detail. "I believe you do not wish to lose my brother," he said finally.

Medair blinked. Did he really think she would lie? When she had already admitted that it had been his tears which had driven her away? Did he think she would be able touch him, if her hate was stronger than the love it had tried to kill? She stared at his statue-still face and realised what a very thin thread was holding that mask of composure in place. Even Ieskar's self-control had its limits.

"And you told me I ran from things."

His face didn't change but his chin lifted, just a little. That was something she'd seen Illukar do, but it was Ieskar who had reacted. It made her feel strange, to see Ieskar react to anything at all, and an immense rush of feeling forced her to snatch at breath. She wanted to do that again, to crack the mask. She wanted to touch.

"I'm not lying," she told him, in a voice which sounded shocked to be genuine. She was trying to imagine Ieskar smiling at her. The very idea made her tremble.

Ieskar just sat there, expression once again completely blank. "Then how?" he asked, at last. "How did you come to love me, Medair an Rynstar? For I saw very well that you hated."

Medair tried to channel all that morass of emotion into speech, to make him understand the feelings which had endured despite her hate, to become the kind of wordsmith Telsen had been. And said, "I don't know." The words fell out and a gasping kind of laugh followed. She shook her head, cheeks hot, and pressed on. "It was an unpleasant shock, when I understood. Hate was a great deal easier, and for a long time I called everything I felt hate, even when it wasn't."

He tilted his head just a fraction to one side. She wasn't sure if he did it deliberately, and decided it meant he was listening. Illukar's grey eyes flashed at her, and she struggled on, face growing ever warmer.

"You are beautiful, Ieskar," she said, with stilted honesty. "And you looked straight through me. And you were so alone." She closed her eyes, dismayed at how wrong that sounded. "I hated the rules which bound you. Could not understand how you stood them. I used to watch your hands turning the marrat pieces. The grace – it, I – I would only let myself think of stopping you. Hating you. I would have used the Horn of Farak on the Ibis-lar. I would have killed you. And it would have–" She looked away, remembering the stinging of the Horn, and the way her chest had seemed to vibrate like a struck gong, when she knew that she had the power to kill the Ibis-lar. "I would have done it, and it would have destroyed me," she whispered.

After a long silence, she lifted her head and stared into those pale eyes, willing him to accept. He seemed to be gazing past her, and she looked over her shoulder at a huge, hazy lake fringed by the border of reeds and islets which had escaped the Blight. Tiny ripples reflected the pale sunlight creeping over the hills, and turned it all into a thing of vast and delicate beauty. It would sparkle at midday and burn at sunset, but in the dawn it earned its name: Shimmerlan.

Ieskar's voice, cool and dreadfully even, inserted itself into this vista: "What would you have done, Medair, if I alone had returned?"

Horrid thought. She turned back to look wide-eyed at him, not even trying to hide her dismay. "I would have mourned Illukar," she said, roughly. "And–" She swallowed the next breath. "And I would have run from you. Frantically." She looked down at the ground, feeling utterly lost. There didn't seem to be anything else to say.

Ieskar stood up. She supposed they would go to The Avenue now, to rest, recover, and shred themselves inside because of the bar which divided them. Slowly, she climbed to her feet, flayed by self-recrimination. She could have lied, she could have told him she was strong enough to overcome her hatred for him alone, to openly be Ieskar Cael las Saral-Ibis' lover. She could have at least tried. When she thought she knew an argument which would convince him, she *would* try. She refused to just give up.

Cool fingers touched her cheek. Teetering into astonishment, Medair looked into ice-blue eyes as Ieskar cupped her face between his hands. He still wore no expression as he traced the shape of her cheekbones with his thumbs, touching her because he could, because there was no longer a law to forbid it, and she had said she wanted him to. Because he had believed her, after all.

She knew she must look stricken, terrified, and lifted her hands to cover his, to declare her desire. Her coward self and her vengeful self could be suppressed. Not hating wasn't one choice, but many, and she would make them all.

His eyes went grey, then blue again. Ever graceful, Ieskar bent his head to her, and paused. He shivered, and that ran through his hands. Then there was the warmth of his breath, and then the tiniest graze against her lower lip. The smallest touch, and it made her blood turn somersaults and ignite. She had not lied to say she wanted him.

Wondering if she could possibly put into words this sudden burning sun, Medair shifted so that they touched: knee, hip, chest. He was still sodden, shirt and skin cold and damp. Her chin grazed his, soft and smooth. So close, she could see in precise detail the way grey flecks rose to crowd out the blue of his eyes. Like a storm of snowflakes, or a hundred thousand butterflies. Then, just as quickly, that ice blue was at the fore, and his lids dropped, a screen of heavy white lashes.

When he moved again, she opened her mouth to meet his, remembering that he had become Kier very young, that the laws which bound him would have meant he would not even have been permitted to touch Princess Alaire, would have had to use magic–

She tasted his lips, and had to grip his wrists tightly because her legs did not seem quite able to keep up with her disbelief. But she did not stop, nor shift away, or even take breath as tentative exploration turned into deep, needy investigation. Hers to touch, hers to taste, to take.

Medair might possibly have stayed there forever, trying to weld her mouth to his, but a distant shout brought an unwelcome reminder of a world outside a white-skinned man with eyes of blue and grey. She quite literally sobbed as she broke from his lips, turned her head only just enough to see the riders.

Islantar, true to his word, had returned for her. At the head of a small unit of guards, he had reined in and was simply staring. Medair thought she had never seen the Kierash look so young.

After another moment, listening to distant peeping, a jingle of harness, and the rasp of breath in the throat of the man who held her, she came back to herself enough to realise that she had her arms wrapped around him again, oblivious to his sorely bruised back. It had to be agonising, but when she hastily adjusted her grip and looked up at his face, she saw no pain, but blue eyes opened wide, almost dazed. Full five hundred years of longing laid bare.

With Islantar and his entourage approaching, Medair was not quite equal to facing those eyes. Not when there was no time to respond. She hid her face in his throat and listened to the tumultuous pace of his heart instead.

There was no need to see blue shift to grey to know it was Illukar who relaxed the death grip about her waist, who squeezed her in quick, silent encouragement before easing back. She caught at his hands, looking up into eyes that were stunned and overjoyed, and even Telsen would not have been able to find a way to say what she was feeling.

"Are you going to tell them?" she asked instead. Her voice was hardly audible. Illukar and Ieskar. She was holding them both.

His eyes shifted to blue. "Islantar will recognise me," he said, quite hoarsely. Speech seemed a thing of long ago. "And I must tell–" He hesitated, shifting to blue-grey, then grey. "–my Kier. But the rest? What gain? I am still Illukar las Cor-Ibis and my memories are my own."

"And Ieskar's."

He half-nodded, then the blue crowded to the surface. Ieskar blinked, and took a breath, then said, "Both," with a little more of his old self-command. "But this is Illukar's life, and I will not appropriate it."

His eyes shifted to grey. "Sharing our life is something we talked of, returning to shore. We cannot suppress each other, would not choose to do so, but Ieskar has no wish for a public face." Illukar looked toward the horses, as a jingle of harness warned that the riders had overcome their initial shock and were hurrying toward them. "Just you," he added, quite seriously.

She touched the mouth which was Ieskar's. It made her ache, suddenly, that she would never really be kissing Illukar's lips again. Just as they would never really return to Finrathlar, but something almost the same. Would he think she loved him only as Ieskar's shadow?

She lifted his left hand, the unscarred one, and pressed it to her cheek. "Can *you* do this?" she asked, anxiously. "You know, don't you, that it's not just– That you and I–?"

But Illukar smiled at her with unimpaired joy. "I know how you looked, when I woke beside you just yesterday," he said. "That had little to do with Ieskar."

"It is still–" She watched his eyes flicker. "I don't want to give you less than everything."

"I infinitely prefer you loving him than hating too much to let us keep what we found together." With perfect formality, he pressed his lips to her forehead. Butterfly light, the kiss still carried a world of reassurance. For, despite everything, they *were* his lips. "I think we're going to be happy, Medair."

She stared up at Illukar's face, with those subtle shifts which also made it Ieskar's. His eyes were grey as he glanced out over the bright expanse of the Shimmerlan, at the blank stretch of water which was almost the fate of all Farakkan. As he looked back down at her, they flicked to blue-grey, and briefly grey as he squeezed her hands. Then they turned to blue again.

Slowly, as if venturing into unfamiliar territory, he smiled.

GLOSSARY

AlKier	The god of the Ibisians, ruler of 'everything' and considered able to manifest as anything, but most commonly depicted as a transparent, idealised hermaphroditic figure visible among clouds.
an	A Farakkian naming custom designating the maternal line. 'an Rynstar' means that Medair's mother was of the Rynstar line.
ar	A Farakkian naming custom designating the paternal line. 'ar Corleaux' means that Medair's father was of the Corleaux line. However, since she was not an acknowledged child of her father, granted heir rights, she should not use the name.
das-Kend	The Kend's second in command.
decem	A Farakkian unit of time a little more than 70 Earth minutes. A single day is divided into twenty decems.
Ekarrel	The form of address given to the Ibisian Kier.
Farak	The incarnation of the continent of Farakkan, believed to have actively created the people who dwell there. Usually depicted as a generous female shape fashioned of fruits and flowers.
Farakkan	A large continent, fashioned into a single Empire known as the Palladian Empire by the Corminevar rulers of Palladium.
Farakkian Farak-lar	People native to the continent of Farakkan.
Ibisians Ibis-lar	The People of the Land of the Ibis. Uniformly tall, pale-skinned and white hair, Ibisians believe that they are by inherent nature 'cold-blooded' (self-controlled). Although they do have a blue line marking their spine, their blood temperature is the same as humans. Their culture is extremely mannered and rigid, with a strong emphasis on following laws and controlling impulse.
Kel	An Ibisian courtesy title for anyone not of the nobility.
Kend	The Commander of the Ibisian armies.
Keridahl	An Ibisian title (translating roughly to 'High Lord of the Cold Blood'). Keridahl command large regions known as dahleins (including Ibsa, Holt Harra, Laskia and Iskand, which maintain a different national identity to Palladium). They often have a particular 'seat' which a Kerikal manages in day-to-day matters, but are expected to spend their time advising the Kier and settling regional disputes.
Keridahl Alar Keridahl Avec	Two Keridahl are designated to sit at the right (Alar) and left (Avec) hand of the Kier, to act as particularly trusted advisors. In the event of the Kier's sudden death, the Keridahl Alar would assume control of Palladium as regent until the Kierash was of age.
Keriden	An Ibisian title. Keriden are an exalted level of Kerikal, controlling the larger cities.
Keriel	An Ibisian title. Keriel control a small area of land (an elein) which may constitute nothing more than a large farm and a single village. [Best equivalent: "Lord of the Manor".] Serves either a Kerivor or a Kerikath.
Kerikal	An Ibisian title. Kerikal rule large towns (somewhat equivalent to mayors). They commonly also hold the title of Kerikath. They owe service to either Keriden or Keridahl, depending on the region they are in.
Kerikath	An Ibisian title. Kerikath command any Keriel and Kerivor which fall within their 'kathilein'. The holders of the title Kerikath usually also hold the title Kerivor, and have their own area of land to manage.
Kerin	An Ibisian courtesy title for male members of the nobility who do not hold a specific title.
Keris	An Ibisian courtesy title for female members of the nobility who do not hold a specific title.

Kerivor	An Ibisian title. Kerivor control a moderate area of land (a vorlein) up to several villages and small towns. May command one or two Keriel. Serves a Kerikath.
Kier	Ruler of the kiereddas. Formerly the Kier went through a binding ceremony to ensure the health of the land, but since the fall of Sar-Ibis this has not occurred.
Kierash	The only title given to an heir, the Kierash is the Kier's designated successor (usually the first-born child, unless the Kier has specified otherwise for reasons of incapacity).
Kiereddas	Previously Sar-Ibis, which was a large, narrow island with no near neighbours. 'Kiereddas' translates to 'the land' and did not originally envisage that there be other lands. The Kiereddas of the Ibisians now encompasses Palladium, Ibsa, Holt Harra, Laskia and Iskand.
las	An Ibisian naming custom indicating the 'clan' the person belongs to. Members of the Cor-Ibis 'clan' are referred to as 'las Cor-Ibis'. The only exception is the current head of the clan, who is referred to simply as 'Cor-Ibis'.
Niadril	A word used to refer to Kier Ieskar after his death. It combines a meaning of 'great', 'eternal' and 'doomed'.
Sar-Ibis	The Land of the Ibis. A large, narrow island with no near neighbours, it was mountainous and fertile, with relatively mild winters. It was consumed completely by a combination of the Blight and earthquakes.

www.ingramcontent.com/pod-product-compliance
Lightning Source LLC
Chambersburg PA
CBHW061213170626
46809CB00003B/1337